CW00449220

REVIVED

Emmy Ellis

Chapter One

The season didn't live up to its name. Although the sun shone, it wasn't exactly Costa del East End at the minute, summer seeming shy to come out in all her naked glory to flash everything she had to offer. It was a bit of a pisser, because he'd selected his outfit based on the weatherman's promise of heat, his T-shirt and shorts now inadequate. Maybe it would warm up later.

Or maybe everyone lied, like *she* did.

He'd found out some interesting things this week by following her. Who she kept company with on occasion (bloody surprising snippet of information there, her meeting The Brothers). The amount of phone calls she had where she walked away to speak in private, glancing around furtively. That she lived nice and *alone*.

He adjusted his holster that held his gun beneath his baggy top. Watched her through binoculars from his hidden spot where she sat in the window of Bumble's Café. She'd arrived by car and parked directly outside, her partner blundering inside after her, the plonker. An odd pairing, her spine-stiff and him slouched. Her on the younger side, him going grey at the temples. Her clearly the one in charge, him meekly obeying.

He pondered on whether he'd do her. You know, offer her a bit of his man sausage. He'd had a couple of women like her. White women didn't really float his boat visually; his first ex was pale, and he'd only gone with her because of being pressured to stick with his own kind. His mother was a cow like that, racist to the core. But if the chance presented itself, would he poke his target's fireplace? Probably. It'd be a free shag. No strings. No choice on her part. The added element of breaking down her stoicism and encouraging her fear to join that party would ramp up his excitement. And he could always close his eyes and pretend she was someone else.

She talked to the man sitting opposite, her expression severe in her concentration to make her point. Her apparent annoyance came across strongly with the jabbing of her finger. He wished he could have gone into the café and sat close by so he could pick up what they discussed. She knew him, would clock him inside a second without his face covered; it wasn't like he could put on his balaclava and go unnoticed.

He hadn't expected today to be the day, receiving the order. Usually, he followed people to see if they were suitable for certain positions, and killed others, swiftly getting rid of anyone who posed a problem, but this one had been followed for a week and had to be interrogated before she met her maker, which meant an abduction and taking her somewhere.

He had to find out what she knew and pass it up the line to the top.

Now, if her partner would just fuck off, he could waylay her when she left the café, but it seemed their breakfast meeting involved hashing something out. Was she reprimanding the fella? Yapping on about any fears she had? Or was *that* conversation only for people who knew *exactly* who she really was? And even then, would she reveal her soft underbelly or remain as strong as she always appeared?

He chuckled at the thought of what was to come. She'd go home at some point today. He'd wait for her light to go off tonight then break in. Slap tape over her mouth to stop any screams. Drag her to the van he'd stolen. She'd never see his face, never know who he was, but she'd hear his voice, one unlike his usual.

The voice of an assassin.

Chapter Two

The uneasy feeling of being watched draped itself over DI Janine Sheldon. As a copper, she was well used to looking after herself, to being alert, more so since she'd taken the role of being bent for the twins. Even *more* so since she'd had the horrible thought that her now-dead colleague, DC Steve Mallard, had told someone in The Network that she still poked that ulcer, was still on the lookout for any police officers taking backhanders from them to pass on information about the case and how close they were, or weren't, to apprehending the mastermind behind the whole operation. De Luca, an Italian man she suspected had an alias he now lived as.

Because she'd had that conversation with Mallard, letting him know she was aware of his part in The Network, he'd had the chance to alert the big boss. She'd stupidly put him on desk duty, thinking she could keep an eye on him until he could be dealt with by the twins, but it wouldn't have stopped him from using a burner phone in the loo to contact de Luca or whoever else his main contact had been now DI Sykes was dead. Mallard must have done so, because when George and Greg went to his house to kill him, they'd found him already dead on his toilet, brain and blood all over the wall—de Luca had clearly deemed him a broken spoke in his wheel. His assassin had left a calling card in blood on the glass shower screen: MINION-215. REST IN PAIN. The code name for Network employees, except they all had a different number.

They'd come after her at some point, she'd said as much to the twins. De Luca would see her as the pesky detective who wouldn't stop until she'd brought the whole organisation down. The fact she wasn't a part of that case any longer, a different team dedicated to it now, wouldn't matter—and Mallard would have told him that. She may still need to be expunged for exposing Sykes and Mallard. Mind you, a couple of months had passed since Mallard's murder, and she'd purposely kept her nose out of Network business lately to save her life.

But what if I've been given a false sense of security and they plan to get me later?

She casually glanced out of the café window so her partner, DS Colin Broadly, didn't think anything was up. She'd just been venting her anger about a case they currently worked on, one her team wouldn't usually be assigned. Extortion wasn't her remit, she was a murder detective, and there were plenty of those in London to keep her busy.

Her thought about the DCI being involved in The Network crossed her mind again as she checked out the people who went about their business as usual outside, going into shops or standing gossiping. Had her boss given her the extortion case, on top of any murders that would inevitably crop up in the near future, to keep her mind from wandering to The Network? His reaction to Mallard being found dead had been extreme. All right, they all took it badly when one of their own copped it, but he'd seemed overly bothered, as if Mallard's death had been more than a boy in blue being taken out.

Or maybe it was her imagination. She was perhaps seeing things that didn't exist.

Not knowing who to trust had been fucking with her mind. Had Colin been chosen to replace her previous DS, Radburn Linton, for a reason? Colin, a man supposedly desperate for retirement and who didn't want to actually work for a living. He preferred Janine to take the lead so he could bumble through his days getting paid for doing the minimal. Had the DCI engineered that so she wouldn't think she was being watched by what appeared to be a lazy bastard?

This was doing her head in.

Spotting nothing out of the ordinary outside, she swung her gaze back to Colin who'd ordered three rounds of toast, even though he'd just hoovered a fry-up down his throat. He paused his chewing to swig some of his Pepsi Max from a can. She sipped her latte.

He swallowed and, can held aloft, frowned at her. "Why are you staring at me like that? Have I got a bogey or something? Bean sauce on my lip? What?"

"Are you on the level?"

"Eh?" He lowered his can to the table and swiped up another triangle of toast.

"Were you assigned to my team to keep an eye on me?"

"Why the fuck would that happen? Are you telling me you're bent?"

"No, not because of that."

His eyebrows lifted. "Jesus, you're not on about"—he inched his head forward to whisper, glancing at the other diners—"The Network, are you?"

"You tell me." She stared at him, hard, and assessed his expression. He seemed genuinely offended she'd suggest such a thing, but she liked to think of herself as a pro in keeping her real emotions off her face, so maybe Colin was adept at it, too.

Or I'm just a paranoid bitch. Maybe I should have taken the twins up on their offer to send someone to shadow me for protection.

"Are you fucking about?" he asked. "I mean, I know you like winding me up, but…"

"I don't know who to trust anymore." There, she'd come clean. Opened up to a partner for the first time in her career. Let him see a chink of the vulnerability she usually kept hidden.

"You think I'm in with *that* lot?" He dropped his toast onto the plate. "I don't know whether to laugh or be pissed off. I'll have you know"—he lowered his voice again—"that I can't even get it up with the missus, even Viagra doesn't help. I've got a problem *downstairs*, so how the chuff am I meant to get it on with refugees?"

"Maybe young women do it for you and your wife doesn't, I don't know. Or maybe that wasn't what I meant. You could refrain from doing anything like that but work for them anyway via the DCI. He could have sent you my way to keep an eye on me. I mean, the case has been passed to a dedicated team that works solely on that now, but our boss oversees it, knows their every move."

Colin flopped back and shook his head. "Let me get this straight. I know I act a div, but I'm not one, just so we're clear. I do it for an easy life. First, you think I'm spying on you, and second, you think the DCI is making sure the bigwigs in The Network aren't caught, is that it? Why would you even *think* that? Is it because Mallard's snuffed it?" He pinched his chin. "What were you *really* talking about with him that day in your office? Was it something other than what you said? You told me you were discussing his career options. That might be true, but *which* career was the main topic? The one with the perverts? Janine, I've got to be honest here, you've bloody offended me by insinuating I've got something to do with people like that."

She wouldn't say sorry. Couldn't. "Do you see it from my point of view, though? Sykes and Mallard were coppers working for The Network. *Both* were killed." Not that she'd admit to him that she'd asked The Brothers to get rid of them. George had killed Sykes, but they hadn't got to Mallard in time. As far as anyone else was concerned, the same assassin who'd gone round killing other members of The Network to shut them up had murdered *them*, too.

"What's really bothering you?" he asked. "Accusation aside—unfounded, I might add— what's getting your goat?"

"They might come after me next. See me as a meddler they can do without."

His frown was back. "Why, though?"

Too late, she realised she'd let her concerns cloud her judgement, rule what came out of her mouth. No one at work knew she'd had conversations with Sykes and Mallard about their dodgy behaviour regarding the refugee situation. Only The Network would know if the two men had reported back that she'd probed them about their involvement.

"Um, why would they think you're a meddler?" Colin pressed.

"Because I was on the original investigation." *Good save?*

"Then that would mean *everyone* working on it has a target on their back, the DCI's being the biggest. Unless, like you've suggested, he's in on it. Stone me, this is all nuts. No one's going to come after you unless they think you're a threat. You're not on that case now, you haven't been shot or stabbed to death, so I'd say they think you're no one to worry about, seeing as you're still breathing."

She finished her coffee in two gulps. Debated whether to let him in on the fact she'd spoken to Sykes and Mallard. "Can I trust you?"

"Err, let me think about that for a minute." He wasn't usually so sarcastic. "Every DI I've worked with as their partner, I've never divulged their secrets. It's all up here." He tapped his head. "And it'll stay there. If you need to talk about something, it'll go no further—unless you confess *you're* with The Network."

She huffed out a laugh. "Unlikely."

"Hmm, we all thought that about Mallard, too. Listen, I've got an exemplary record, I've worked bloody hard, and now I just want to kick back for the remaining years I have left in the job, but if you want to become buddies rather than just colleagues, that's fine by me. Think about it. If I was in with The Network, I'd have a damn sight better house than the small one I live in, and I sure as shit wouldn't shop at Aldi, forgo having holidays because funds are tight, and I bloody well wouldn't still be in this job, waiting for my copper's pension." He held a hand up. "Before you say it, yes, I could be playing the long game, not spending Network cash so it doesn't draw

13

attention, but I'm not. I never have, and never will, be a bent copper. So yes, you can trust me."

"What are your thoughts on bent coppers?"

He shrugged. "If they turn a blind eye to certain things to save all that paperwork and it doesn't really affect people that much, like old Hilda nicking a tin of tomatoes, I can handle that. But if we're talking proper bent, then they should be ashamed of themselves and shouldn't be in the job."

That solved her issue of whether to come clean about working for The Brothers. He'd likely grass her up to their boss if she opened up there. Down on paper, her crimes would appear hideous, and no one would understand how she felt that having the twins ridding the East End of scum was actually doing everyone a favour. She was supposed to uphold the law, not encourage people to break it.

Yet here we are.

"I need to tell you something," she said. "It's because I'm worried about my safety, and if something happens to me, you'll know why. You might actually *see* me as bent once I tell you the story, but you have to understand I wasn't sure about Sykes and Mallard until they wound up dead." *Liar*.

Colin swept his gaze around the café. "We should continue this conversation in private. Fuck knows who's listening."

Is that because there's a bug in my car and what we talk about in there will be on record?

She almost laughed at her paranoia, but stranger things had happened.

"We'll go for a walk, our phones off," she said.

"Fuck me, you think I'd *record* you? Whatever you're involved in, Janine, I've got no clue about it. Either you want to talk or you don't. Christ, you can even frisk me for a wire if you want. Come on."

He picked up his Pepsi and walked out. A sense of slight relief rushed through her, although she stopped herself from fully relinquishing herself to it because he could still report back to the DCI verbally.

She caught up with him halfway down the street. At the end, they turned into New Road and, a few houses along, veered into an alley between two council homes that led to a park. A few mums with little kids occupied the play area, and Janine steered their direction to the picnic tables. Colin placed his can, phone, shoes, and watch on one of them, then marched over to another, too far away for the items to pick anything up. She'd clicked why he'd removed his footwear—he could have a device in his shoe heel, and he wanted to prove he was trustworthy.

He held his arms out, legs apart. She approached him, did the frisk, checked all of his pockets, then sat.

"Feel better now?" he asked, sitting.

"A bit, but you could still go running to the boss about what I've said. I'll deny it, just so you know."

"Well, *that* doesn't sound dodgy, does it." He rolled his eyes. "Right, out with it, then."

She took a deep breath. "After we'd discovered the refugee house and had gone inside, I caught Sykes paying particular attention to the bedding in one of the upstairs rooms."

"Oh. And we know why now. His DNA was found on a sheet."

"Right, but at that moment in time, I didn't particularly have any suspicions about what he was doing. I had a word regarding his handling of storming the house, how the timing didn't match. Basically, I gathered that he'd manipulated it so anyone inside who worked for The Network could get away once they knew the police had arrived. Anyway, it came about that he basically admitted being involved. I assumed he'd been sleeping with the women." She'd assumed more than that, but Colin didn't need to know. "I gave him a warning that he should cover his arse, that the sheet he inspected might get him in the shit, which it did, although he was dead by the time the results came through." Now came the outright lie. "Before Sykes died, I went over and over it in my head as to whether I should tell the DCI that Sykes had sex with a refugee, whether to encourage Sykes to tell him himself, but when I'd made my mind up to pass the information up the chain, Sykes was killed."

"So you feel guilty that you didn't speak up in time."

"Yes." *No.* "Then I have the extra guilt about Mallard."

"What about him?"

"You were right to suspect I wasn't talking to him about career options at work. I'd put two and two together when it came to my attention that a woman called Marleigh Jasper had—"

"Hang on. Came to your attention? How?"

17

She forced a blush. Prepared another lie. "I'd been poking into Sykes after he died. On the quiet. I wanted to find his link to The Network. I remembered him and Mallard whispered a lot sometimes, shifty glances an' all that, so I poked into Mallard, too. Marleigh Jasper had spoken to *both* of them regarding the Polish woman who'd tried to get help in Golden Glow."

"Zofia Kowalczyk."

"Yes. Neither of them had followed it up, it wasn't in the records that they'd paid Goldie a visit, and I asked myself why. So I called Mallard in for a chat."

Colin raised his eyebrows. "And?"

"He said he couldn't recall why it hadn't been followed up, reckoned he must have been too busy, so I pushed him on it and brought up Sykes." *More lies to follow…* "Mallard said Sykes had told him he'd dealt with it and not to worry."

"When? I mean, the timeline isn't adding up. I had to sift through Mallard's records after he was murdered, remember, and he didn't speak to Marleigh until *after* Sykes had died."

"Exactly what I said to him, which means they'd previously discussed Sykes' involvement in the *original* call Marleigh had made, way before she phoned in again. It rang alarm bells, so I told him if he was also involved in The Network, he needed to go back to his desk and pen his resignation then explain himself to the DCI. As we know, he was killed before he chose to do that, so it left me wondering whether he'd told de Luca about me prodding him about Sykes and Marleigh, so de Luca had him offed for possibly being a liability."

"You obviously haven't told our boss about those conversations."

"No."

"Why not?"

"Because I fucked up by keeping it to myself all this time. He'll want to know why I didn't go to him immediately after I spoke to Sykes in the bedroom and Mallard in my office."

"Why didn't you?"

Lie, lie, lie. "Call me naïve, but I didn't want to believe they were involved, they were good detectives, and then when it became clear they were both up to their armpits in it, it was too late for me to come forward. I worried the DCI would think *I* was involved with the organisation, too, for not reporting them."

"I see your point. But now *I* know, so *I've* been put in a position."

"Can you pretend I never told you?"

Colin leant his elbows on the table. "I don't know, Janine... I mean, I don't want to risk losing my pension if it comes out I knew this and didn't say anything. But at the same time, I get how these things run away with you, how we keep our mouths shut sometimes."

"Like old Hilda with the tin of tomatoes."

"Well, yeah, but this is slightly more serious than that."

"Telling the DCI serves no purpose now. Sykes and Mallard are dead. They can't be held to account for what they did. I can, yes, but if I promise myself to go straight to the boss in future..."

Colin nodded. "Is that a proper promise, or are you just trying to fob me off?"

"A proper promise. Col, I could be next, do you see that? Sykes and Mallard will have told de Luca about me badgering them."

"Look, you'd be dead by now if he was that bothered." He stared at the sky. "But this brings us another dilemma. What if the DCI *is* involved and he wants you kept alive? What if he's persuaded de Luca to leave you alone because two dead coppers already shows the rest of us in a bad light? A PR exercise, preventing people thinking, even more than they already do, that our division is corrupt."

"Bloody hell…"

Colin sighed. "What a can of worms." He fiddled with his fingers. "The main thing here is to make sure you're safe. How long has this been bothering you? Like, do you feel watched? Have you spotted someone following you?"

"It's bugged me ever since Mallard's murder. And I felt watched in the café earlier, but I looked out, and no one seemed suss."

"I'd say you're safe if they haven't got to you yet. Can't you go and stay with someone?"

"How long for? It's been two months since Mallard was bumped off. And I could still get hurt, or killed, wherever I stay; if I'm being watched, they'll know where I go. If they decide I'm to be taken out, they'll just do it. Look how they've done it to everyone they've wanted to keep quiet so far."

"I'd say speak to the boss, but now you've got me wondering if he's dodgy. Shit."

"There's no way to get word out to let The Network know I'm not a threat."

"Then it's a case of sitting tight and hoping nothing happens."

"But if it does, and I don't turn up for work one day…" She thought of her burner phone, the one she used to contact the twins. Christ, if she wound up dead, unless her killer disposed of the mobile, the whole force would know she worked for them and her name would be tarnished. She'd have to have a word with George and Greg, warn them that if they couldn't contact her at any time and they suspected she'd been murdered, they'd have to ditch their own work burner. They were pay-as-you-go efforts, but best to be safe.

"What do you want me to do if that happens?" Colin asked.

"Keep what I've told you out of it and act as shocked as everyone else. I don't expect you to become more involved than you already are by knowing my concerns."

"If you don't want me to do anything, then what's the point in me knowing?"

"All right, here's the bottom line. I don't have any friends. I don't have anyone who'd *care* that I'm gone. I've told you so someone *does* care." The twins would, but they weren't exactly bosom buddies, and the only real reason they'd give a proper shit was because they'd be without a bent copper on their books for a while until they found a replacement.

"What about your family?"

"Strained relationships."

"Sorry to hear that."

"Hmm."

He scratched his head. "So now we've established you've been a numpty a couple of times by not reporting your colleagues, and that doesn't matter now because they ended up dead—I'm going with the Hilda's tomatoes thing on that—we need to deal with the bigger issue. Can you afford to have security put on your new house? Like an alarm?"

She'd moved last week to Roland Avenue, thinking a change of address would throw The Network off, which was stupid, because they might have been following her. "Probably. I've got some savings." *But the twins will pay for it.*

"Then get it sorted. Now." He poked a finger towards her. "Come on, get your phone out. Ring round and book something before we get called out to another bloody murder."

23

She took her burner phone from her pocket, one he'd likely think was for personal use. Made a show of looking up numbers on Google for security companies. Held her mobile up so he couldn't see she wasn't putting a number into the keypad, even though her finger moved as if she was. Instead, she jabbed the GG icon, the only name in her contact list.

"What's up?" George asked.

"Good afternoon. Is that Cyborg Security? Oh good. I was wondering if you could fit an alarm at my place before the end of today."

"Is this a fucking wind-up?" George asked.

"No. I *need* an alarm, and your company has the best Checkatrade reviews."

"Right. Yeah, we can do that."

"So I fill out a form, you say?"

"Err, yeah?"

"You'll want my email address, then." She rattled it off. "Is the form so you have my address and everything? Makes sense. How does this work? Shall I go home and wait for you, give your men my keys? They can leave them in the electric box outside once they've finished, so long as they set the alarm before they go."

"We don't need keys. We're handy with picks."

"I realise that."

"Ah, you're with someone?"

"Yes."

"Sorry. Bit short on the uptake this morning. Is there anything we should be worried about?"

"Lovely. We'll talk later, then. Thank you." She switched the phone off and slipped it away. "Okay, that's that sorted."

"You'll sleep easier. At least you'll get a warning if someone breaks in."

But it didn't solve the issue of her being assassinated elsewhere, though, did it. She was alone when she picked Colin up for work and after she'd driven him home. Those were her vulnerable times. If it wasn't for her incessant gut feeling since Mallard's death and the sense of being watched at the café, she'd forget all this, but something was off its axis, and it didn't take a rocket scientist to work out that her ego, inquisitiveness, and utter stubborn streak had led her to this.

And she had no one to blame this time but herself.

Chapter Three

*F*ourteen-year-old Becky Sutton stood in front of Mr Tomlinson's desk and squeezed her hands together. Nerves always got to her with this teacher. He emanated a weird vibe, as though beneath his professional veneer lurked a darkness that he fought to keep hidden—a deeper darkness than he already showed everyone anyway. He was already abrasive *and rude, especially to her and anyone who didn't have the same colour skin as him.*

Daksh Gupta sat at the back, waiting for his turn to get told off. Everyone else had gone to the next lesson. Becky didn't want to be reprimanded in front of Daksh, but it wasn't like she had any choice. Mr Tomlinson called the shots, and she was just some kid he needed to get in line, or maybe, as she'd long suspected, he wanted to manipulate things so she was eventually expelled and he wouldn't have to deal with her anymore. She was a good kid, but he didn't like her, always choosing her to clean all the paintbrushes after art class, never anyone else. Daksh had the constant job of washing out the pots. It wasn't fair, and today she'd kicked up a fuss about it. He hadn't been too happy, accusing her of showing him up in front of the other students, ranting and raving, asking her who she thought she was.

Someone else had said that recently, to her mother, as if Mum standing up for herself wasn't allowed. Mum had sucked her teeth and told the neighbour to go and attend to her own business instead of sticking her nose in theirs. Becky had remembered that incident as soon as Mr Tomlinson had ordered her to collect the brushes, and it had been on the tip of her tongue to tell him to mind his own business, too. Instead, she'd

28

asked, politely, why it was always her. He hadn't answered at the time, just shouted about her being rude and whatnot, then told her she had to stay behind, but she had a feeling he was going to now.

"In reply to your earlier question," he said, "if you want the God's-honest truth of it, it's because you're black."

Daksh sounded like he choked on something, his cough echoing—at least she had a witness—but her breath stalled in her lungs, the room seeming to buzz with the silence that followed that cough, all three of them suspended in this odd void she didn't want to be in. The air had a sour redolence, maybe the result of her armpits breaking out in sweat in the overheated room. Then the clonk of the too-hot radiator brought her back to life.

She blinked. No stranger to people making reference to her skin tone, she was still shocked a teacher, of all people, had said it outright. She should have expected it from him, though. She'd already noted how he singled her and Daksh out, and before he'd left the school, a black lad, Kelvin James, had been picked on, not only in art class, but if Mr Tomlinson saw him elsewhere on the grounds, he homed in on him.

Becky wasn't going to take this anymore. "That's racist."

The teacher shook his head and tutted. "Ah, that old chestnut. Will you people ever stop that nonsense?"

You people. She'd heard that before an' all. A derogatory term to make her feel inadequate, less than, and she was sick of it. Her usually placid Mum would go mad when she heard about this—anything bad like this set her off. She'd come up here and rant, pointing in his face and telling him a few home truths about his fellow man, how they were oppressors, some of them monsters, and he should be ashamed of himself.

"I won't stop telling people when they're being racist, no," she said and stiffened her spine. Daksh was Indian, and she was sticking up for him, too, and for the absent Kelvin. "You getting me to clean all the brushes because I'm black is wrong."

He sneered, his nostrils flaring. It appeared, with her challenging him, that the deeper darkness wanted to come out. Would he be able to control it? Hold it back?

"Wrong to you, but not to me." He took a long breath, perhaps trying to rein it in, then it was clear he'd come to a decision—a bad one. He glanced at Daksh then back to her. "You're slaves, every one of you. And as for your lot"—he flapped a hand towards Daksh—"with your stinking curries…" He stood. Planted his palms on the desk. Gritted his teeth. "Now

30

then, if you've quite finished your little speech, Sutton, I suggest you mind your manners."

What the hell? No, he had not *said that.*

But he had.

She narrowed her eyes at him. He was being an arsehole, giving in to his base self, maybe thinking he'd get away with it because of his position of authority. Was she just going to take this? No. But what could she do about it?

She held back a smile and thought of how much trouble she could get him into if she…

"Can I leave now?" She didn't add the required 'sir'. He didn't deserve any respect.

"I just said to go, didn't I? Now get out of my sight."

Then he added the N-word.

Daksh choked again. "Oh my God, *sir!"*

"Shut your Paki mouth, boy."

"I'm Indian!"

Becky paused, blinking once again at how rude Tomlinson was. How he thought his privileged arse had the right to say that to her and Daksh. Mum was a kind woman, always trying to see the best in others until they proved they were past saving, and she'd once said that some people couldn't help being racist because they'd been brought up that way and it was all

31

they knew. It didn't excuse it, though. Dad had argued that everyone had their own minds, their own thoughts, and they could stop being nasty if they really wanted to.

Mr Tomlinson was past saving, and he deserved all he got.

He laughed at her pausing, enjoying her shock. "I said, get out of my sight!"

She walked to the classroom door, unable to look at him. She didn't want to see his wide smile, his eyes glittering with hatred for 'her sort'. In the corridor, she peeked through the glass in the door, and Daksh scratched his head, frowning as if he couldn't believe what had just happened. Why *didn't he believe it, though? They were always being picked on by that man.*

Enough was enough. She marched down the corridor to reception, waiting in front of the secretary's desk for her to notice she was there.

Miss Marchant stopped typing, raised her head, and smiled brightly. "Ah, Becky, what can I do for you? Aren't you supposed to be in class? The end-of-lesson bell went ten minutes ago."

"Mr Tomlinson kept me behind. Can I speak to Mrs Guttenberg, please?"

Miss Marchant frowned. "Oh, did Mr Tomlinson say you had to?"

"No."

"Hang on, let me see if she's available."

She went off to knock on the head's door. Opened it and poked her face around it. A quick conversation, too low for Becky to pick up, and then she gestured for her to come over.

Becky entered the office, nervous; she always was when she had to see Mrs Guttenberg, because it was usually Mr Tomlinson who had sent her here for one reason or another, usually based on lies. He claimed she didn't pay attention or she disrupted the class, which she didn't. It was all in his warped mind.

Mrs Guttenberg, about sixty with grey hair, glanced up from behind her steel-rimmed glasses and shook her head. She sighed. "What have you done now, Becky?"

Becky closed the door and went to stand in front of her desk. She shook, but she couldn't keep this to herself any longer. "I want to report Mr Tomlinson for being racist."

Mrs Guttenberg widened her eyes. "Take a seat. This is a serious allegation. What, exactly, did he say? Are you sure you didn't just take his words the wrong way?"

Becky automatically added 'like you lot always do' in her head, because that's what people generally said. Or had she imagined the head would say something like that? Yes, she had. Mrs Guttenberg had never given her any indication before that she wasn't an inclusive person. In assembly, she regularly gave talks about equality.

This was what Becky lived with, day in, day out: constantly working out whether someone was a closet racist or not. Whether they were genuine, kind. It was exhausting.

Becky sat, her hands trembling. Not from fear but anger. "No, I heard him properly."

"What did he say?"

"I asked him why he always gets me to clean the paintbrushes, and he said it's because I'm black."

"I beg your pardon?"

Becky opened her mouth to repeat herself, but Mrs Guttenberg lifted her hand.

"No, no, I heard you. It's just… Dear God…" She stood, paced, a finger to her chin. "What else did he say?"

"That I need to mind my manners. Then he called me the N-word."

"What?" Mrs Guttenberg stopped pacing and came over to Becky. She held the tops of her arms and bent

34

slightly to look into her eyes. "Listen to me. No one should call you that word, you know that, don't you? It's not acceptable."

"That's why I'm here, Miss."

Mrs Guttenberg let her go and went to a wall planner. She drew her finger along it. "Mr Tomlinson has a free lesson now, which is the perfect time for us to have a little chat. Come on. I'll sort this out."

"I don't think you can, Miss. He's nasty to me all the time. And to Daksh."

"Daksh Gupta?"

Becky nodded. "Here's there now, getting told off."

"What for?" Mrs Guttenberg took Becky's hand and led her out of the office and through reception.

"He said Daksh stinks funny and needs a lesson in personal hygiene, and that's why he's being kept behind. He also said about curries being smelly." She bit her lip, tears stinging. "He called him a Paki."

Out in the corridor, Mrs Guttenberg paused in leading Becky along and leant against the wall. Her eyes watered. She turned to Becky. "I'm so sorry you had to go through that, but I'll fix it, I promise you."

"Is that because you'll get in trouble if you don't?" Becky hadn't been able to stop the words from coming out. She wasn't stupid, she knew how the world worked. People had to be seen as not being racist, but

35

they still could be underneath—and often were. Mrs Guttenberg wouldn't be allowed to brush this under the carpet, she had to act or likely be given the sack. Mind you, those tears of hers…they seemed genuine.

"Absolutely not," the head said. "I'm doing this because it's right. He shouldn't be marginalising anyone."

She led the way again, Becky following behind. A slither of fear went through her. What if Mr Tomlinson denied it? What if Daksh didn't back her up? And even if he did, Mr Tomlinson was such a spiteful person he could say they were both lying, that they'd made it up.

The closer they got to the art classroom, the sicker she felt.

Then Mum's voice piped up in her head, and she felt better. "We're going to make a difference, girl. We are, I promise."

Mum had joined a group where they spread awareness about racism, and she had the ear of the local journalist who stood in solidarity with them. It had worked better than they'd thought, and at least to their faces, the mean people in their street and those surrounding it didn't give them filthy looks or treat them unfairly anymore. It was a start, so Mum had said, and Rome wasn't built in a day, but one small brick at a time, they were going to knock down that wall.

She'd be proud of Becky for doing this.

At the art room door, Mrs Guttenberg peered through the glass and gasped. Becky nosed to see what was going on. Daksh, face pressed against the wall, Mr Tomlinson at his back, stared at them, tears running down his cheeks. His arm, held up between their bodies, was at a painful angle, and Becky's eyes stung again.

"Oh my God," Mrs Guttenberg shrieked and threw the door open. "What on earth do you think you're doing to that student?"

Becky flinched. 'That student' was just as bad as 'your lot' or 'you people', only the head probably didn't realise it. Many people didn't understand the undertones of what they said. How could they, when they hadn't had to live with what Becky and Daksh did, and all the other people who weren't white? Becky told herself the head was coming from a good place, that she sounded disgusted and shocked, so that counted for something, but 'that student' had separated him in some way just the same. Made him something 'other'.

Mr Tomlinson stepped back from Daksh, his cheeks flushing.

Mrs Guttenberg approached and took Daksh's hand. "Come away, son. Are you all right?"

Son. Becky had to blink tears away at that. Mrs Guttenberg wouldn't have said it if she thought the same way as Mr Tomlinson, would she?

Daksh wiped at his cheeks. "My arm's a bit sore, Miss."

Mrs Guttenberg didn't seem to know what to attend to first: Daksh, Mr Tomlinson, or the racial slurs. "Do you need the nurse?"

Relieved the woman had gone with the correct decision, caring for Daksh first, Becky let out a slow breath.

Daksh shook his head. "Nah."

"Have a seat just here." Mrs Guttenberg guided him to a chair and stepped back to waft a hand at Becky, asking her to sit beside him, her smile one of apology and also: *I see you. I know now, and it will be all right.* "Mr Tomlinson, please can you explain what you were doing to Daksh?"

"I was teaching him how to defend himself. Some horrible boys have been picking on him, a dreadful business, and he needed advice. We were acting out a scenario where he was waylaid in the dark and—"

"That's not right, Miss." Daksh stared at their teacher. "You were saying how people like me should *go back to their own country. How you hated us. How you wished we'd been drowned at birth."*

Mrs Guttenberg appeared ready to explode. Her hands trembled. "Is that true, Mr Tomlinson?"

"Err, no. He's got quite the imagination, that one."

"Like I have?" Becky said, standing. "Did I imagine you calling me the N-word and Daksh a Paki?"

His cheeks grew redder, but he laughed, if a little unsteadily. "Now then, young lady, we all know you're prone to exaggeration…"

"I heard you," Daksh said.

Mr Tomlinson clasped his hands down by his groin. "I assure you, Mrs Guttenberg, that this is nothing but a ploy, cooked up between the pair of them, to get themselves out of trouble. Becky, especially, is a troublemaker. Look how many times I have to send her to your office. Both have behaved appallingly in my lesson today and—"

"Do you have a problem with other races?" Mrs Guttenberg asked bluntly.

"Of course not! That would be abominable."

She stared at him. "I'm white. But I'm Jewish. Do you have an issue with that?"

His face hardened for a moment, but it was long enough for Becky to recognise he'd revealed his distaste. He was a white supremacist, that much was obvious.

"I'll schedule a meeting with you for a later date," Mrs Guttenberg said, her words clipped. "For now, I'd like you to go home. I need to go through the proper channels before we proceed."

Mr Tomlinson glared at her. "I'm being sent home because these two...these two...young people are lying?"

Had he been about to slip up there and call them something nasty again?

"We'll discuss everything in due course." Mrs Guttenberg patted Daksh's shoulder for him to stand. "I'd like your desk cleared within half an hour, Mr Tomlinson."

She led Becky and Daksh out, Becky wondering whether Mrs Guttenberg should have said all that in front of them. She'd basically suspended the bastard, and maybe that should have been done without them there, but God, it had been good to witness it. What it proved to Becky was that the issue itself was more important than any protocol the woman had to follow.

"I'm going to speak to my solicitor about this!" Mr Tomlinson blustered from behind them. "I'll not be accused of saying those words! It's tragic when the word of two...children are believed over an adult."

In the corridor, Mrs Guttenberg paused and looked into the classroom. "Perhaps your solicitor will also furnish you with a copy of the twenty ten Equality Act, because by the sound of it, you need to read it."

She closed the door and clip-clopped down the corridor.

Becky glanced at Daksh who pulled a face. Then they smiled and went after their saviour, Becky giddy inside because she'd taken a brick or two off that wall Mum was so intent on breaking down.

She'd done the right thing.

Hadn't she?

Chapter Four

Becky took a deep breath and knocked on Debbie's flat door. She didn't even know if the woman would be in, but she was tight with The Brothers and might pass a message along so Becky could meet them. If she was out, maybe Lisa downstairs in the pub could help.

Anxious someone would see her, considering she stood at the top of steel steps on a landing at the side of The Angel, she ducked her head. When she'd walked along the street pushing her baby son, Noah, in his buggy, she'd clocked the sex workers standing at the top corner past The Roxy nightclub, but none of them had paid her any mind, nor had a man in the alley opposite. All the same, she was paranoid someone watched her.

She clutched a sleeping Noah to her chest, having left his buggy beneath the stairs. His father, Lemon, was the reason she'd come here. He'd left her a while back, his mother, Faith, telling her he was well shot of her. Becky received no child support. But despite that, it wasn't the sole reason she'd come here. Lemon had told her a few things he'd been getting up to, and keeping it to herself wasn't an option any longer. She'd held off for as long as she could, but she had Noah to think of, and if the twins found out she'd known and hadn't done anything…

She didn't want to die, although they might kill her today anyway. The rumours that went round about them frightened her, but she'd talk herself out of death if she had to. Or hope they were in a good mood.

44

She knocked again, praying Debbie just hadn't heard her the first time. A lock clunked, and Becky straightened up. The door opened a little, a chain preventing it from being pulled back fully, and a face appeared in the gap.

"Hello?"

"Sorry, you don't know me," Becky said, "but I need your help."

"You're not a corner or parlour girl, so…"

"I know. I need to get in contact with The Brothers. I have information and —"

"Hang on." The chain disappeared, and the door opened wide, revealing Debbie in pink Lycra sportswear and Skechers trainers.

"Oh, are you off to the gym? I could come back…"

"Yoga, I'm trying out 'me time' for a change, but it doesn't matter. I farted there last week doing the downward dog, so I could do with leaving it another week before I have to see that lot of prissy cows again." She nodded at Noah. "Will he need feeding or anything? I ask because you haven't got a changing bag, and the twins might not be able to get here for a while if they're busy."

"Oh. Um, yes, he's due a bottle in about an hour. I'll just go down and get the bag. I left it in the bottom of the buggy."

Debbie poked her head out and looked across the street. "I'll go. You get inside." She stepped back to allow Becky in. "I won't be a tick."

Becky went in, standing awkwardly in the hallway while Debbie's footsteps thumped on the stairs.

A minute later, Debbie appeared with the buggy. "In case you want to put him in there to sleep while you have a cuppa." She plonked it on the floor, closed the door, and chained it. Bolts across, she scooted past Becky. "Come through."

Becky laid Noah down, wondering why Debbie felt the need to barricade herself in during the day. Becky would probably never find out, so it was pointless thinking about it. She pushed the buggy into a kitchen.

Debbie stood at a Tassimo machine inserting a pod. "Coffee or tea?"

Becky parked the buggy beside a breakfast bar and lingered, unsure whether or not to sit if she hadn't been told to. She decided on coffee, even though she'd prefer tea; she didn't want to put the woman out too much. "Whatever you're having is fine, thank you."

"That's a latte. Park your arse. I'll message the twins in a minute. What do you need to speak to them for? I'm not being nosey, but it's guaranteed they're going to ask me."

"My ex. He's...he's been doing things he shouldn't."

"Oh right. Who's he, then?"

"Lemon. Do you know him?"

Debbie winced. "Who doesn't? He's a twat. Comes in The Angel sometimes with his mates from Sparrow Road."

"That's what I need to speak about. They don't just live in Sparrow Road, if you see what I mean. They call themselves the Sparrow Lot."

"Oh, a *gang*? Bless them..." Debbie chuckled. "That'll soon get stamped out." She passed a cup, spoon, and a clicky thing of sweetener over. Then she popped another pod into the machine, placing a mug beneath. "Right. I'll ring them now." She grabbed her phone from beside the microwave.

Becky's stomach rolled over. She was doing it, getting Lemon right in the shit, and while it was a good thing, she was still frightened. Plus, seeing the twins after they'd posted five hundred quid through her letterbox a couple of months ago, them knowing she'd stolen nappies and bread from Yiannis at the corner shop, well, it was embarrassing. She'd explain. Say sorry.

Debbie related what Becky had said, nodding. "Okay, see you in a minute."

Becky blew on her drink then sipped. This was all happening so quickly…

"Are you okay?" Debbie put her phone down.

"Just a bit nervous."

"What, of The Brothers? They're pussycats."

"To you maybe."

"I suppose." Debbie sorted her drink then leant her backside against the sink unit. "Are you involved in anything to do with Lemon and the Sparrow blokes?"

"God, no. I had no idea he was into anything like that until he told me."

"Then you'll be all right. How long have you known?"

"A couple of months."

Debbie pulled a face. "Ah, that might get them shirty. George and Greg don't like it when people hold stuff back."

"I know, but the more I thought about telling them, the more I convinced myself they'd kill me."

"How old's your baby?"

"Five months now."

"Are you coping all right?"

Becky shrugged. "It's hard on my own."

"I bet. Emotionally as well as financially. Is that why you're here, to get a payout for information?"

"I'm not going to lie, I could do with some money, but that isn't the only reason. I want to get back at Lemon, yes, but the shit he's involved with…it needs to stop."

"I see." Debbie cocked her head. "That was quick. They must have been in the area because they're here already."

The sound of footsteps on the steel stairs had Becky's anxiety ramping up, so she busied herself with drinking while Debbie went to let them in. When they returned, Becky put her cup down, her hand shaking too much to hold it steady. She couldn't tell which twin was which, they dressed the same, even down to the red ties, so she nodded to both, shame heating her cheeks that they knew she was a thief.

"Bloody hell," Debbie said, squeezing in past the one who blocked the doorway. "Shift your fat arse, George, will you?" She stopped in the middle of the kitchen. "Bugger me, I didn't even ask your name, love." She smiled at Becky. "Sorry."

"Rebecca Sutton. Becky."

George stepped closer. "I looked into you after the bread and nappy thing. You're a relation to a certain copper."

Becky nodded. "My aunt. Sheila. I know, you don't have to say it. She's white, I'm black. She's married to my dad's brother if that helps explain things."

"I know. And your skin's got fuck all to do with anything, I just mentioned a relation, it was you who brought that up."

"I find I have to on account of people drawing attention to it—and seeing as I stole nappies and bread, some would say they'd expect that from 'my kind'." She rolled her eyes.

"We're not 'people', we take as we find, and loads are out nicking at the moment because they can't afford to fucking feed themselves, so you're not alone. And don't be ashamed. It's all squared away with Yiannis anyway."

"Thank you. And for the money."

"Not a problem. Now then, what's this about? What have the blokes in Sparrow Road got do with anything?"

George sat next to her. Greg leant against the wall beside the door, staring down at Noah, a small smile forming. Did he want children of his own?

"Come on, then," George prompted. "Let's hear the goss."

She launched into what she knew, and at the end, said, "He told me a couple of months ago, and although I wanted to tell you sooner, I was scared."

"Of?"

"You killing me."

George laughed. "Understandable, given our rep, but even if you *had* said something back then, we were a bit tied up with something going on at our casino so wouldn't have been able to deal with it right away. We know now, that's the main thing, and seeing as you're shit scared of Lemon, we can give you a pass on not coming forward sooner."

Relief ploughed into her. "He left me not long after he spilled the beans because I wouldn't stop going on about it. And I got to thinking of all the times he didn't come home. Stayed away for days, his phone off, and I assume it was because he was doing jobs for the Sparrow Lot. Or he was seeing another woman. His mum said he's better off without me. She was smug about it, too."

"Why be smug?"

"She didn't say, but I caught the gist. I'm black, she'd prefer me to be white like them. She's dropped enough hints for me to understand her take on our relationship. She told me once to go back to where I came from. I said I was already there, was born here, but she sniffed and walked off. I think that's why she's never taken to Noah. When we took him round there after he was born, she said she preferred purebred cats, but I knew what she was really saying."

Greg grunted. "She needs her fucking mouth punching so she can't say shit like that."

George nodded. "I'm game."

Something silent passed between the twins, as if there was some understanding there regarding what they'd just said to each other. Too wired to try to work it out, Becky shrugged it off. She wasn't going to die today, her being black wasn't an issue, and they were going to sort Lemon and the Sparrows.

"How are you for money? Lemon paying you for the baby?" Greg asked.

"No, he isn't."

Greg drew in a long breath through his nose. "Wanker."

George dipped in the inside pocket of his jacket and brought out two envelopes. He slapped them on the breakfast bar. "One is for your information, the other is for your boy. Later down the line, if you need shit for him, you come to us. He won't go without, understand?"

"Yes."

"I mean it. School trips in the future, clothes, whatever."

Tears brimmed. "Why are you being so nice?"

"Because kids should never have to go without, go hungry, and their mothers shouldn't have to suffer the consequences of being with a dickhead. You two won't suffer like some did." He glanced at his brother, and another silent message passed between them. "We'll look after you both. You can even work for us if you like."

"I've got a job. I'm on maternity leave."

"Do you like it? The job?"

"Not really."

"What would you prefer to do? Come on, if you could do anything in the world, what would it be? Our mum, she didn't get to choose her path till she was much older, so we're giving you the chance to start now. Tell me."

"I don't even know."

"Have a think, and when you know, we'll be listening. I can't promise a supermodel gig or anything like that, but within reason."

She swallowed down emotion. "Okay."

"So will Sheila pose a problem, her being a copper an' all that?"

"She doesn't know I'm here. I haven't told her anything because that's what Lemon would expect, and he'd get himself out of any shit because he's clever enough to have alibis. It'll be his mother, she'll say anything he tells her to."

George smiled. "She won't be saying anything once we've fixed her gob."

Debbie snorted. "I'm guessing you won't be using your fist."

George laughed. "As it happens, no."

Becky didn't ask what he'd use. The less she knew the better. Faith wasn't exactly on her Christmas card list, and from the moment she'd been treated unfairly by Mr Tomlinson, she'd vowed never to let a racist have space in her heart. She'd never allowed herself to hope Faith would accept her. Whatever happened to the woman wasn't her concern. Did that make her a bad person? Did caging her emotions with certain people mean she was wicked if she didn't give a shit what happened to them? Shouldn't she care for *every*one?

It was difficult to when *she* wasn't cared about sometimes.

"What happens now?" she asked.

"You go home and act normal. We'll be in touch."

A horrible thought barged into her head. "But what if Lemon twigs you're onto him and he comes round to mine?"

George glanced at Greg again.

Greg pushed off the wall. "How do you fancy a little holiday?"

Becky hadn't expected that. "Err, where to? And I can't afford one, so talking about it is pointless."

"You don't need money." Greg crouched to look at Noah. "Our mate's got a chalet in Southend. It's used for instances like this. All that sea air will do the little one good, and you'll be safe while we sort Lemon."

She nodded. "That would be lovely, thank you."

"Do you drive?"

"Yes."

"Then we'll arrange for you to go tonight." Greg stood. "I'll carry the buggy downstairs for you, then we'll be in touch with the Southend address. We'll need to swap numbers."

They got on with that, Becky bemused with how life changed, just like that. When she'd woken up this morning, she hadn't thought she'd be sleeping by the sea tonight. No, she'd thought she'd have had a bollocking off the twins and would lie there crying, wishing she hadn't bothered contacting them.

"It'll be all right, you know," George said. "You've got us now."

Chapter Five

The afternoon had turned hot, a far cry from this morning when it had been more like early spring. The sun had burnt off the early morning chill, and the clouds had all fucked off, leaving the sky a pristine blue.

Lemon kicked a nearby car tyre in frustration and paced the quiet backstreet. Things with the Sparrow Lot had been getting out of hand lately.

The 'boss', Capo, as he liked to call himself, used Lemon as his right-hand man, sending him off to do all the things he didn't fancy doing himself — but taking the glory when shit went the way he'd planned. Lemon was sick of being the one to pull things off and Capo getting the back pats, the adoration. He wanted things to return to how they used to be, before he'd involved himself with the Sparrows, but he hadn't been given the green light for that yet. He doubted it would be coming anytime soon either.

In other areas of his life he was the top of his profession, and it suited him down to the ground, dishing out orders and people obeying. His mum, Faith, was a prime example of how to get someone to blindly do whatever you wanted, as was Leia, his first ex-girlfriend, although Becky… Shit, he'd fucked up by going with her. Not only had she got herself pregnant — what a div — giving him a kid he didn't want, but she'd turned into one of *those* women who expected him to tell her where he'd been and what he was doing at all times. She'd even asked him to help with the fucking *housework* when she'd come home from hospital after Noah had been born. Who did she think he was, a 'new man' who was in touch with his feminine side? Fuck that, he wasn't about to do any washing up or run the hoover round if he didn't have to. That was women's work, and men should only do it if they lived without a bird on hand.

He waited for a phone call to come through. Had left a pint on the shiny bar at the new gastro pub the twins had just opened, Noodle and Tiger, because a message had come through saying he needed to go somewhere private to answer it. Juggling the various aspects of his life had become more difficult of late because he'd taken on more than he had in the past, what with the Sparrow Lot. Ditching Becky had been a weight off his shoulders, though. Her constant picking at why he stayed away from home sometimes, why he was never *present*, even when he *was* at home, had forced his hand, and he'd used the Sparrows as his excuse.

It wasn't like he could admit to who he really was.

Fuck me, she's got no idea who the hell I am.

He played several roles. Lemon, the gobby twat who acted hard with the Sparrows, a man who seemed to want to make a name for himself, when really, it was just a cover; the son, who told his mother to jump and she asked how high; and the assassin, who sometimes had to hide away in a designated flat for a few days after he'd killed people.

Minion-66.

A couple of months ago, he'd killed a copper, Mallard, for his boss in The Network. A loose end, he'd been told. Weren't they all? Now, he had a new target, DI Janine Sheldon, who'd been poking a little too hard into coppers who'd been employed by The Network. All the other pigs working the case weren't people the boss was worried about—someone on the police team ensured the investigation went in directions away from the organisation. But Janine, who wasn't supposed to be nosing into things that didn't concern her anymore, had taken it upon herself to root out the bent coppers, Sykes and Mallard.

That was a laugh, she was bent herself. Had something going with the twins, or so Lemon had gathered, what with her meeting them last week under the arch behind the warehouses. Unfortunately, he hadn't been able to go close enough to hear what they'd spoken about, but an envelope had changed hands. Maybe they'd given her a tip-off. Or maybe she was on their payroll. Those phone calls she got, where she acted furtive... Were they from The Brothers?

He'd find out after he'd snatched her from her bed later.

He'd followed her to the park earlier but hadn't gone into the nearby trees to listen in. One, he'd have been spotted, and two, Capo had phoned him unexpectedly, wanting him to pick up a stash of cocaine. Normally, while on a Network job, he gave it his sole attention, but with de Luca's order for him to ingrain himself in Sparrow life until The Network could come back out to play properly, he'd had to do as Capo had asked. It didn't matter, he'd done the main reconnaissance with Janine, and everything was in place there. Now he could get back to his shenanigans with Capo—thinking of a way to bring down the twat in their gang who'd taken it upon himself to sell gear on another estate.

Lemon thought of Goldie, the leader who'd gone missing a couple of months ago. Lemon had gate-crashed his party at the social club, telling him someone was selling on his patch without permission, and he'd secured a meeting with him for the next morning at Golden Glow to discuss

Goldie getting rid of the pest for them. Lemon had turned up at the tanning salon, only to be told by some woman called Babs that Goldie wasn't answering his phone and he hadn't arrived for any of his meetings.

The next thing Lemon knew, some ponce called Prince Judas had taken over The Golden Eye Estate, renaming it The Judas Estate to match his own. Lemon had requested an audience with him, surprised when it had been granted. He'd passed on the news about Dipsy selling drugs (the Teletubby name suited him; he had a pot belly and liked the colour green), and Prince had said he'd deal with it.

Had he eff. Dipsy continued to sell on Judas. Off his own bat, Dipsy had cut a deal with the leader, which ate into the profits, meaning everyone in Sparrow got paid less. So guess whose job it was to go after Dipsy and get rid of him? Lemon had the perfect cover to disguise the fact it was a gang-related murder by using his Minion-66 gun. But should he dare to do that when de Luca hadn't sanctioned the murder? And it might get into the papers that the bullet used matched the striations of the ones found in the bodies of people Lemon had dispatched for

The Network. Capo would know Lemon was an assassin then, and that wasn't supposed to get out.

Unless…

He nodded to himself. Yeah, he could get around that issue.

At last, his Network phone rang, and he answered. "Boss."

"I wanted to speak rather than message," de Luca said. "I happen to be in London. There are several jobs for you, and I need to show you their pictures."

Lemon understood why. All email communications had been halted since the police had discovered The Network existed. No images were sent in WhatsApp anymore either. De Luca used code words to give orders now, ones only the Minions could read via a translation app, but for the boss to have the brass neck to come back to London must mean the targets were too important—or on the verge of spilling the beans about The Network—for Lemon to be given names only, risking him taking out the wrong people. While he thought de Luca was a dickhead for coming to London, putting himself at risk, so long as he got paid, what did he care?

"Where do you want to meet?" he asked.

"I'll be with you any second."

What?

The line went dead.

Lemon turned at the sound of an engine. A sleek black Mercedes crept down the road. It stopped beside him, and he opened the back door. Got in. He wasn't even freaked out that he'd obviously been followed here for de Luca to know where he was. Nothing the boss did would surprise him.

Lemon stared to his right. De Luca appeared nothing like the boss he'd met before. Gone was the dark-haired, suave Italian, and in his place sat a distinguished-looking man with a barnet of grey, a matching beard, and his eyes changed from brown to blue—a creepy, chilling blue that people would remember.

The car pulled away, the peak-hatted driver behind thick privacy glass.

"Fuck me, I wouldn't have recognised you," Lemon said.

"That's the idea." De Luca passed an envelope across. "I need all of them taken out by tomorrow; they are clients, men who bought women. They are on the verge of talking. This, we can't have, can we."

"How did you find out?"

"One of them pretends to be like them. He has joined their 'boys' club', but he works for me. He was asked to attend a meeting, where they discussed sending details to the police anonymously tomorrow afternoon, giving names of Network employees. They don't intend to say they are in possession of refugees who they have locked up in their homes. Hypocrites. If it wasn't for me, they would not have their playthings."

"Why would they want to do that? Grass us up?"

"They appear to have grown a conscience. Of course, you won't allow them to continue breathing in order to bring us down."

"No. They'll be gone by tonight."

"I expected you'd say that. You always work fast. As for the women...they will be moved on after you have let me know each man has been taken care of. We have a new house ready for when we start to bring fresh meat into the country. They will go there."

"What about Janine, though? I was supposed to collect her tonight."

De Luca shrugged. "Who knows, you may still have time. If not, get her tomorrow night. My source says she's been quiet since Mallard. She hasn't been poking into anything, so for now, she's got some extra hours of life to live."

Lemon thought about his Dipsy dilemma. "I wanted to ask a favour. Can I use my gun to kill someone from the Sparrow Lot?"

De Luca turned his weird blue eyes Lemon's way. "What for?"

"I need a cover as to why he's been killed. Capo doesn't want it looking like he ordered him to be bumped off."

"This Capo…he thinks he's an Italian boss like *me*?"

"No, it's just his way of being called boss, so he's different. You know he's a twat and just a means to an end. He's sod all to worry about. Like I told you, Prince hasn't dealt with Dipsy for us like Goldie would have, and Dipsy's still selling gear on Judas, shafting the rest of the Sparrows in the meantime. I'm juggling balls at the minute by being involved with Capo and his lot."

"I'm sorry, but it was necessary for you to be seen as a little gangster man so no heat came your way. You're my biggest asset with regards to murder, my best assassin, and I couldn't risk you being caught. So yes, use the gun. People will think he was a pervert, a man who had sex with the refugees, or someone employed by The Network—actually, I'll make sure my contact in the police puts that into their colleagues' heads. It will give them a false direction to go in, so be prepared to be questioned by them, seeing as you're Dipsy's 'associate'. They'll want to know if you knew what he was up to."

"Cheers."

"I want the men in that envelope dealt with first, though."

"Understood."

The driver had taken them on a jaunt and now drove back down the road where Lemon had been picked up. The bloke must know exactly how long de Luca's conversations would take, or maybe de Luca had some weird thing going on where he made eye contact in the rearview mirror to give him instructions.

"Do you want me to hole up in the flat after I've sorted the men, Dipsy, and Janine?"

"Not this time. You must continue with the Sparrows and this Capo, as people will notice you disappearing now. The money will be left at the flat, though. Collect it during the night."

Lemon nodded and got out. He sat in his van, waited for the Merc to fuck off, then opened the envelope. Four males, all of them over forty. Names and addresses on the back of each one. He memorised them, then popped the photos in the envelope. He drove to Mum's, and seeing as she was at work, burnt the envelope and its contents in a saucepan, then flushed the ashes down the loo.

He sent a message to Capo.

LEMON: GOT TO GO TO SOME STUPID BOOK CLUB SESSION WITH MY MUM THIS EVENING. DON'T EVEN ASK, MATE… IF I SAY NO, SHE'LL GET ARSEY. WILL CHAT ABOUT MY THOUGHTS ON SORTING DIPSY TOMORROW.

CAPO: A BOOK CLUB? WITH YOUR OLD DEAR? FUCK ME… [LAUGHING EMOJI]

LEMON: I KNOW, SHE'S A FUCKING WASTEMAN. TALK SOON.

He washed out the saucepan and put it away. Kettle on for a coffee, he thought about his plan of action tonight. How well de Luca had disguised himself. How, if the Italian wanted, he could end Lemon because he knew too much.

He'd even been entrusted with the boss' real name. Lemon had earnt that trust, had proved time and again he could be a ghost in the night— or day—killing people who could bring trouble to The Network's door, all for tidy sums he stashed away for the time he could buy his own gaff.

There was another reason why he'd got in with the Sparrows. Becky had been getting suspicious about him staying away for days on end when he'd holed himself up in The Network flat after he'd followed employee recruits or murdered people. Months later, and he'd told her he ran around with the Sparrows and what they did, thinking it would shut her up.

It hadn't. She'd gone on and on, saying he shouldn't get involved in illegal stuff, and he'd had no choice but to leave so he could get some peace and quiet.

He hadn't wanted a proper relationship with her anyway, had only used her from the start as a cover for what he did for de Luca. He'd have been seen as finally settling down, no one to look at in terms of being a killer, but then she'd got up the duff, and while that could be the perfect cherry on top of the 'disguise his real life' cake, it had affected him personally. Emotionally. Mentally. He wasn't *ready* for a fucking kid.

Fuck her, and fuck that baby. The pair of them were anchors.

His phone rang, startling him.

What the chuff does he *want?*

One of the Sparrows, Baba Vanga (he reckoned he could predict the future, the prick, and acted like an old woman sometimes, so the nickname had stuck), had been keeping an eye on Becky since Lemon had left her but so far hadn't had anything to report. She lived the life of a typical single mum, struggling to make ends meet, not going out with her mates, and generally looking like a scabby dog. Was Vanga going to tell Lemon something, today of all days, when he had so much else to do?

Fuck's sake.

His two lives converged in ways he didn't like. Gone were the simple times of being just Minion-66.

"What?" he barked on answering.

"Jesus, who's pissed on your pudding?"

"Sorry, I'm annoyed because my old dear's dragging me to a fucking book club tonight, of all things."

Vanga laughed. "You poor bastard. And here I am, just about to knob you off even more."

Lemon sighed. "What's Becky done? I assume it's about her."

"She visited The Angel today."

Lemon rolled his eyes. "So? Maybe she fancied a bevvy, although I'm surprised she can afford one." He chuckled. What a loser she was.

"She went to the flat upstairs."

That wiped the smile off his face. "*Debbie's*?"

"Yeah."

Lemon thought about that. Was she after a job? As a *prosser*? He cracked up laughing at the thought. She'd need lessons in sex if she was going take that on. Useless in the sack, she was.

"What's so funny?" Vanga asked.

"Just imagining her asking Debbie for a job."

"Jesus. You won't be laughing in a minute. Five minutes after she went in, The Brothers turned up."

"*What*?" Anger, so fierce, sluiced through Lemon's body, and he punched the worktop. "Are you fucking me about?"

"Nope. They were there a while, then left. Becky came out ten minutes later and walked to

71

that little shop down by her place. Came out with a load of shopping bags."

"She's skint, so how could she afford that much shopping?"

"Think about it, bruh. She must have got a loan off them. You know how George likes to help out the povvy people lately, like he's some kind of do-gooder messiah. Don't forget that Greek prick, Yiannis, was extolling George's virtues that time because he put money on someone's leccy. Anyway, she went home. She's still there."

"Christ, she must be boracic if she's turned to the twins for dosh."

"Can't she ask her mum and dad?"

"They got naffed off with her keep asking, said it was up to me to provide for her and the brat."

"Still want me to watch her?"

"For the rest of the day and tomorrow, yeah, see if she goes and parks herself up on the corner dressed as a tart. And take a picture if she does so I can have a laugh about it."

"Aren't you bothered where Noah will be when she's spreading her legs?"

"Why should I?"

"Well, he's your kid."

"So she says."

"Christ..."

"Yeah, I reckon she was playing away behind my back. Anyway, cheers for the info."

"I'll get back to you if anything else happens."

"Yeah." Lemon jabbed the END CALL button and examined his feelings. No, he didn't care, not about Becky going begging to George and Greg, being a prosser—or about that son of hers.

He had more important things to think about.

Chapter Six

*C*harlene Tomlinson and her group of mean friends stormed towards Becky and Daksh the next morning during break time. Sitting on the wall surrounding the netball court, Daksh beside her, Becky took a deep breath. Mum had warned her there would be backlash from grassing on Mr Tomlinson, and it seemed it was coming their way.

"You got my dad suspended, you fucking pair of cunts." Charlene stopped in front of them, hands on hips, her blonde ponytail pulled back tightly, unsanctioned eyeliner thick.

Now Becky had a chance to study her up close, she saw the resemblance. Charlene had the same beady eyes as her father, the same sneering lips. "He got himself suspended. Why should we take the blame for someone else's behaviour?"

That's what Mum had said, and it had stuck in Becky's mind. She had to remember this, always, that her skin didn't mean people could do and say whatever they wanted to her or anyone else, as if them being white gave them the divine right.

"There's going to be a disciplinary meeting," Charlene went on. "He could lose his job. My mum's ill, she can't work, so how the fuck are they meant to pay the bills?"

"He should have thought about that before he opened his mouth," Daksh said. "He shouldn't have been racist. Even if he thinks those things, he could have kept them to himself."

Charlene glared at him. "What do you know, you Paki piece of shit."

Becky couldn't help her gasp, which matched a couple from two of Charlene's friends. One of them,

Laura, turned her back, to distance herself from the situation, as if that meant she played no role in this, but turning away was part of the bigger problem. Not doing anything concrete to stop this crap was on a par with actually doing it—the same as joint enterprise with a murder; you may not be the one delivering the fatal blow, but you were complicit. By standing there quietly, not voicing your concern or giving help, strengthened the mortar that held those bricks together. Silence equalled acquiescence.

Daksh sighed. "I'm not from Pakistan. You need to educate yourself."

Charlene huffed. "On what?"

"Cultures, all the other peoples, all the races—and know the difference."

"What do I need to do that for? I don't care who the fuck you lot are, you don't belong here. Like my dad says, you should all go home."

Becky sighed, too. This was the same old, same old bollocks. "We are *home. We were born here."*

"Then your mums and dads need to fuck off and take you with them."

How many times had Becky heard this bullshit? "They were born here, too."

Charlene frowned. Clearly tried to compute this. Or was she dredging up some kind of response that justified her behaviour? "Well, you people had to come from somewhere."

Becky glanced at Daksh: Is she for real? "So you don't even know where we 'came from' or why?"

"I don't need to know. The fact you're here when you shouldn't be is enough."

Becky tried to get her to see. "My grandparents came from Jamaica. Look up about the Windrush Generation. Like Daksh said, you need to educate yourself."

Charlene's face clouded. "But if they weren't here, your nan and grandad or whatever, then you *wouldn't be here. You'd be climbing up trees and being savages instead, throwing spears with bones in your noses and all that weird shit."*

Wow. I didn't imagine that, did I. She really said that?

Laura whipped her head round to look over her shoulder, the shock on the visible side of her face clear. She swivelled her whole body slightly, looking at Becky, and for one of those moments everyone had, where words were spoken without anything being said, time suspended. Laura broke the spell and walked away, then she ran. The others remained, glancing at each other behind Charlene's back—it was obvious even they'd realised Charlene had gone too far. How brainwashed she was. How mean.

"You need to walk away now," Becky said.

"Why? Going to act the tough girl and hit me, are you? Or are you scared of me?"

Becky was glad to find she wasn't. Although anger burned inside her, she actually felt sorry for Charlene, whose mind was so closed it had a welded-shut padlock on it. "Nope. The only thing I'm scared of is that you'll likely pass your beliefs on to others, to your innocent children, adding to the layers of hatred that are already there."

Charlene leant closer. "Well, you should be scared, because I'm going to fucking bury the pair of you for what you've done to my family."

"For what your dad *did," Daksh said.*

Charlene gritted her teeth. "He stood up for himself. Tells it like he sees it. What's wrong with that?"

"If you can't see what's wrong with it, then that says everything," Daksh said.

"And what does *your dad see?" Becky asked, already knowing the answer.*

"A load of wogs and Pakis who don't belong. There's tons of you around here now. Fuck me, I can't go anywhere without seeing one." Charlene tsked. "You'd best watch your back, bitch. And as for you,

Mr Curry, keep out of my way." She flounced off, her cronies going with her. "Where the fuck's Laura gone?"

Becky looked at Daksh. "Laura's in for it."

"Hmm."

"We should go and see Mrs Guttenberg." Becky stood.

Daksh nodded ahead. "No need. She's over there."

Becky shifted her eyes. The headmistress stalked towards Charlene and her friends, closely followed by Mr Reynolds, the geography teacher.

"Christ, they're in the shit now," Daksh said.

Becky smiled. "Good."

Everyone hushed. It wasn't every day there was an emergency assembly. To have been called out of lessons and instructed to sit quietly and listen, really listen, hadn't happened since Felix Enstone had been stabbed by another student. He'd died on the pavement and had done nothing wrong.

Mrs Guttenberg's last sentence echoed: I want to educate you. "In nineteen forty-two, a ship, the Monte Rosa, was seized by the Nazis to be used in the deportation of Norwegian Jewish people, of which I am *a descendent. It was turned into a prison ship. Below deck, cages were put in place to house prisoners who were split into groups of men and women, then divided by age. They ate nothing but thin porridge and watery soup. Put yourself in their place. Can you imagine being incarcerated like that, fed appalling food, and crammed into a cage with others, the air stifling, all because you were Jewish? When they arrived at their destination, Hamburg, they had guns pointed at them and were forced to board wagons. They were taken to Auschwitz. You have already been taught about that, so I don't need to go into details about the horrors."*

No one said a word. Becky picked up on the multitude of breaths, how the majority of the children seemed to understand that this was a serious, serious talk.

"Later, in nineteen forty-five, the Monte Rosa *was taken by the British and renamed. That ship became the* Empire Windrush. *By nineteen forty-eight, British Caribbean passengers, who were citizens of the British Empire, arrived for a new life. They were qualified people, finding it difficult to secure jobs at home, and they came to England for work. Think about how you would feel, having to leave everything you loved behind. I want you to take a moment to really imagine this. Your bedrooms, containing all your*

precious things. Your friends, some of your family. The streets you play on, the house you live in. You pack a case and board a ship, heading for a place that is so different to what you know. Your identity is stripped and morphed into something else—something many people in our country imposed on you. You're 'different' now. As they used to say back then, you're 'coloured', as if that's a dirty thing to be. Everything you ever knew, all of it, gone, and you have the daunting task of trying to fit in, a new life where it's clear you're not wanted."

Feet scuffed the floor. Were the kids feeling uncomfortable? Sad? To have the truth thrown at them, when they may have been taught differently by their parents...were they confused? Wondering whether to believe their families or Mrs Guttenberg? Asking themselves if they'd been lied to by the very people who should always tell them the truth?

"Imagine again, that when you've arrived in a country you thought would welcome you, you discovered MPs, eleven of them, wrote to the then Prime Minister and asked for a halt, and I quote, 'to the influx of coloured people'. How would you feel to know you weren't wanted? How would you feel, to read in a certain newspaper, that an assumption was made based on the way you dressed?" She lifted a piece of paper. "This is what was printed. 'There were even emigrants wearing zoot-style suits—very long-waisted jackets, big padded shoulders, slit pockets and peg-top trousers.' This assumption was that those arriving shouldn't be here if they could afford such clothing and the fare from their homeland—that they would be taking jobs British people could have had. A suggestion that the 'influx' prevented others from having a job. The same goes on today, fruit pickers and NHS workers looked upon as thieves of work."

Becky had known it wasn't just her and her family, other black people who suffered, of course she did, it was a big part of her life, but that last sentence expanded her mind even more and showed that so many people were treated unfairly, as if they all didn't belong to the human race and were somehow a different species—as different as a giraffe from a fish. It hurt her heart that this was so deep-seated, so prevalent. Still, despite the laws.

Mrs Guttenberg cleared her throat, visibly upset. "Imagine again, that when you got here, you couldn't find accommodation, the availability of which was diminished due to the war, and you were sent to an air-raid shelter. Think about that. An air-raid shelter. When you went into shops—if indeed it didn't have a sign on the door that said, 'No blacks'—you were stared at, called names. Made to feel ashamed of who you are. You long to return home, because no one treated you differently there, but you're here now, in a whole new world where some people make it clear they don't like you. This disgusting trait has continued right up until this day, only people aren't allowed to openly voice those feelings anymore. Marginalisation isn't tolerated. Why then, do some people feel it's okay to express the teachings of their parents and grandparents? Remember, we are not born racist, we are created."

Becky thought of Mum. She'd said that.

"But it doesn't excuse it," Mrs Guttenberg went on, echoing Becky's dad. "In no circumstances is it okay to voice racism." She paused. Consulted her notes. "Also in nineteen forty-eight, the first people from India arrived. Lured here by the promise of work to help rebuild Britain after the destruction of World War Two, Commonwealth citizens were given free entry. Along with other countries' inhabitants coming here, we became a diverse and beautiful country — that is how we should look at it. We should embrace every culture, every religion, every person — as a human being, not because of their skin tone."

Students waited for the hammer blow, because one was coming, Becky could feel it. Excitement raced through her to be a part of this, to experience how it felt to actually get something done, like Mum did in her group.

"I have told you stories of only three instances of immigration—there are so many more we could discuss, and we will, once a week from now on, for the next six weeks. The reason for this emergency talk is that racism has reared its ugly head here this week, in our school, where we pride ourselves in equality and inclusion. Many of you do, too, but some don't."

Someone gasped. Another coughed.

Mrs Guttenberg cast her gaze over all present. Teachers, standing to the side, looked repulsed that racism had been an issue, especially Mr Reynolds, who'd obviously witnessed a dose of Charlene's views after he'd escorted her and her friends to the head's office earlier. Mr Tomlinson popped into Becky's head. What was he doing now? Seeing that solicitor? Reading the Equality Act? Or was he sitting at home, seething, plotting how to get himself out of the mess he'd dumped himself in?

The headmistress carried on. "Only this morning, at break, I have had to suspend five students—one for outright vile and spiteful words, the others for standing there, complicit, doing nothing to stop it. I will not tolerate this kind of behaviour. I want *everyone to learn about emigration and immigration. Each of you will be required to write at least one thousand words on the subject and hand it in by this time next week. I want you to learn compassion—and to unlearn latent, or outright, racism. Anyone found to be using derogatory words or actions towards anybody in this school will face suspension or even exclusion. Always, always, put yourself in someone else's shoes before you open your mouths. Have I made myself clear?"*

Becky glanced across at Laura who blushed and dipped her head; she must at least have done a U-turn on her views if she'd gone and grassed Charlene up, or maybe she hadn't agreed with Charlene in the first place but had been too scared by peer pressure to stand up and say it was wrong. Almost everyone else appeared to understand the gravity of the situation, but James Stockport sneered and shook his head. So he'd been raised to believe certain people didn't belong, that they didn't have the same rights as him.

It was then that Becky knew she'd be battling this fight for the rest of her life.

And it crushed her.

Chapter Seven

Becky arrived in Southend-on-Sea late afternoon. The chalet, a little wood-clad bungalow, its roof slate, had an open-plan setup for the living room and kitchen, a bathroom behind a door to the left, the bedroom to the right. The twins must have passed on her needs for Noah, as a travel cot stood beside the double bed, and a packet of nappies and wet wipes had been provided along with a bit of basic shopping: teabags, milk and the like. She'd been to Yiannis' shop earlier to get a few bits using the money George had given her, and she looked forward to a total break away from London. To forget the past few months and retrain her brain, as she'd been advised by Debbie.

"Take it from me, the past can rule you if you let it," she'd said. "*Don't* let it. *You're* the one in control, not what happened before, and certainly not people like Lemon and his mother."

Noah, ready for their stroll, slept in his pushchair. She left the chalet, locked up, and took the short walk to the beach through the town. It looked much the same as when she'd been here as a child, and she was surprised she remembered the way. She stopped and took in the view. The sand, the huge estuary that led to the sea. The pier. Mum had told her once it was over a mile long. People sat on the beach, some with large parasols, others with pop-up tents for shade. While it was coming up to dinner time, it was still packed, everyone taking advantage of the sun. She'd come back to the beach tomorrow, see how Noah liked playing with the sand, but for now, she wanted food. She walked to Pavilion

Fish and Chips with its circus tent appearance, the big-top roof striking with its red-and-white stripes.

With the package still wrapped up, she headed for the pier, strolling down it, the people at the nearby Adventure Island shrieking on the roller coaster, the Ferris wheel turning slowly. She opened up the package and rested it on the hood of Noah's pushchair. The scent of salt and vinegar wafted up, and her mouth watered. Why did fish and chips smell so much better at the seaside?

She ate as she went, letting the water either side of her give the impression she was free of tethers, reducing her life to nothing but her, the sea, and Noah, until someone else went by, shattering the illusion, or the train, *Sir John Betjeman*, clattered past, its blue carriages bisected with a white stripe down the middle. Gulls cried out overhead, and by the time she'd reached the end of the pier, she felt as if she'd entered a new world. She meandered around, taking in the view and smiling at people casting off their troubles.

On the way back, Noah woke and wanted a bottle, so she paused halfway along and sat under the covered seating, thankful he'd stopped his 'I want food every two hours' malarkey he'd settled into when he'd been younger. She fed him, changed his nappy, and sat him on her lap for a while, people smiling at him as they walked by, one woman pausing to chat, mundane rubbish about the weather, but Becky welcomed the conversation.

Another train came by, *Sir William Heygate*, and she put Noah in his pushchair and continued her walk back. At the chalet, she bathed her son and got him ready for bed, playing with him for a while to tire him out. He went through the night now, another thing she was grateful for, and she looked forward to putting him in the cot and having a glass of wine in the peace and quiet.

If only every day could be like this one, where she offloaded her issues onto someone else and they took care of it, sending her for a holiday so she was safe. But she had to return to London at some point and could only hope the Sparrows didn't come for her after Lemon had been dealt with.

Before the twins had left Debbie's, George had mentioned 'sorting' him, and she wasn't sure, but it sounded as if it translated to 'killing' because Greg had been appalled at how Lemon had treated her, not to mention her ex doing things he shouldn't on Cardigan. She hadn't wanted to discuss it—didn't want to be culpable just by knowing. She'd been through that situation before, and it still haunted her. All she'd asked for was that they stopped Lemon from doing what he did with the Sparrows, and possibly persuade him to pay her child support.

She thought about their job offer. What *would* she do if she had the choice? She still didn't know. Maybe that was something she could ponder when she went to bed, staring at a strange ceiling.

Chapter Eight

Ichabod had been temporarily relieved of his managerial duties at the twins' casino, Jackpot Palace, to go and follow some bloke called Lemon. To begin with, as far as he could tell, the man was nothing but a scrote and lived with his mother who'd gone out late morning, presumably to work. Later, Lemon had driven to a backstreet and loitered on the pavement for a bit. He'd kicked a car tyre, and Ichabod had made a mental note that the fella might have a temper. A Merc had turned up, one with blacked-out windows, and Lemon had got in. Ichabod had followed at a discreet distance, and on their return had waited for the Merc to go before he'd parked in a spot on the opposite side of the street. Whoever had picked Lemon up had given him something. Through his binoculars, Ichabod had seen Lemon looking at it, or maybe it had been his phone. The Merc's number plate had been sent to the twins, and Ichabod had tailed Lemon home.

Now, at eleven p.m., the summer sky finally going to bed, Ichabod sat in another stolen car with fake plates outside a big house in a cul-de-sac. The five other homes, spaced wide apart, were of the posh variety. Clearly, people with money lived inside them, their vehicles all gas-guzzling SUVs or sleek, expensive makes. Unlike when he'd used Marleigh Jasper's house to stake out Goldie, he didn't have to be at a higher level to view the homes. None of them had six-foot hedges or iron-barred gates surrounding them. Instead, they stood on large, landscaped gardens, topiaries dotted here and there along with flowerbeds and pruned shrubs.

Lemon had gone round the back of number two, his outfit suggesting he was up to no good — all black clothing, a balaclava disguising his features, night-vision goggles covering his eyes. Ichabod had sat here for three minutes so far and decided his Irish arse would be better off round the back, too. He slid his own balaclava on, took his gun out, and left the car, creeping along the cul-de-sac to number two.

Down the side, he held his breath, let it out, then rounded the corner, gun raised. The back door stood ajar, and, cautious, he entered the property, standing in the dark beside a long breakfast bar, careful not to nudge any of the stools with his foot. A soft *pfft*, a sound he recognised, had him following it to the source. In the unlit hallway, he peered through the gap by the hinges of a door. A lamp cast Lemon in a soft glow — and a man who no longer owned one side of his head. Blood and brain matter dotted the cream sofa beside the older fella whose expression appeared serene in death, as if any shock he'd experienced had faded from his face in the seconds after he'd taken his last breath.

Ichabod retreated quietly and left, returning to his car to update George and Greg.

ICHABOD: THE FECKIN' EEJIT SHOT SOMEONE IN THE HEAD AT THE LOCATION I UPDATED YOU WITH. HOW TO PROCEED?

GG: FUCK ME. DON'T DO ANYTHING TO INTERVENE. I'LL SEND WILL TO WATCH THE HOUSE AFTER LEMON'S GONE TO SEE IF ANYONE COMES TO REMOVE THE BODY. FOLLOW HIM AGAIN.

ICHABOD: DID YOU FIND OUT WHO OWNS THE HOUSE?

GG: JANINE HAS JUST GOT BACK TO US. SOME BLOKE CALLED EVAN PARKINS WHO DOESN'T RUN IN LEMON'S KIND OF CIRCLES, SO IT LOOKS LIKE LEMON'S A HITMAN. NEVER WOULD HAVE THOUGHT IT. KEEP US INFORMED.

Ichabod responded that he would and tucked his phone in his pocket in case the twins messaged back. The last thing he needed was his burner in the cup holder lighting up and giving away the fact someone sat in a car, watching.

Lemon coming from the side of the house had Ichabod putting his seat belt on, ready to go after him. He'd keep well back, and wherever Lemon went to next, Ichabod would continue past so the man didn't get suspicious, then park farther up the street and spy from there.

Taking another deep breath, he observed Lemon getting into a black SUV and easing away from the kerb. Lemon hadn't used the van he'd pootled around in earlier, and Ichabod suspected the SUV's plates were false.

What was he doing? Offing people for the man known as Capo? The Brothers had passed on Becky's story, and by the sounds of things, Lemon wasn't such a lemon after all, he was a stone-cold killer. What would the Sparrow Lot have to do with a man like Evan Parkins, though? Why would they want him offed? The Sparrows were rough and ready men in their twenties and thirties, had nothing in common with someone who lived in a gaff like this.

"And there was me thinking he was an eejit. Wonders will never feckin' cease," Ichabod muttered and followed the man out of the street.

Will sat outside number two in a small van and stared in shock at what was going on. Two men in dark clothing carried a gagged woman across

97

the front garden and put her inside the back of a Transit, one of them getting in with her. The other drove them away, and rather than waste time messaging the twins, Will went after them.

He enjoyed working for The Brothers, mainly surveillance jobs, many of them boring, but this one was proving to be an eye-opener. Out in the sticks between estates (Cardigan and Moon), the Transit turned onto a track set in the middle of some woods, and as Will passed, he just made out a house in the distance at the end, the squares of light from windows pinpricks in the dark. He continued on, then veered into a lay-by half a mile or so away, taking his phone out.

WILL: THEY'VE CARRIED A WOMAN FROM THE CUL-DE-SAC AND DRIVEN HER TO ANOTHER HOUSE.

He added the location, then waited.

GG: WILL LET JANINE KNOW. GO TO THE ADDRESS I'M GOING TO SEND YOU, WHERE LEMON AND ICH ARE NOW, AND SEE IF THE SAME THING HAPPENS.

WILL: RIGHT.

Will drove to the place just as Lemon and Ichabod left a street full of four-storey Victorian townhouses that must have cost a packet. They cruised by, and Ichabod acknowledged Will with a slight nod. After about fifteen minutes, the

Transit came along and parked outside number sixty-three. The front door had been left open a little, and the two men entered, closing it. Five minutes passed, then they emerged with another gagged woman.

What the fuck was going on?

WILL: SECOND WOMAN BEING REMOVED. I'LL CHECK IF SHE'S TAKEN TO THE SAME PLACE AS THE OTHER ONE.

GG: JESUS.

Will drove behind them, staying back a bit, hoping they didn't twig the same car had followed them twice. When they turned onto the track, he kept going, once again parking in the lay-by.

WILL: SAME PLACE. NEW REFUGEE HOUSE?

GG: DON'T KNOW. JANINE CAN LOOK INTO IT. STAND BY SO YOU CAN GO TO WHEREVER LEMON AND ICH END UP.

Will smiled, anticipating what was to come. Tonight had turned into quite the interesting job.

Chapter Nine

Lemon had shot three men so far, and with one to go, he checked the time to see if he could squeeze in abducting Janine. Midnight had arrived, so he reckoned he could swing it. Night-vision goggles on, he left the car in a lay-by and approached the house via the expanse of grass next to a long drive, trees either side of it festooned in fairy lights. It bugged him that people either didn't bother taking their Christmas decorations down or they'd decided having those lights was a good idea. It was dumb in his opinion, and especially here, where the drive resembled a runway, letting everyone know a house stood at the end, ripe for burgling.

It belonged to a Mr Johnson, the first host of a new thing for The Network—a sex party, where people had dressed up to the nines and watched others having it off, maybe joining in themselves. Before the old refugee house had been discovered, the women had performed on a stage here, and two had escaped. Stupid to have had the refugees at a party with so many people. It was obvious, with the amount of exits and guests being otherwise engaged, that at least one of them would make a run for it. De Luca had attended the party, as had Denny, the man who'd run the East End refugee house, yet neither of them had kept an eye on the stage and noticed two women were missing until the alarm had been raised.

Sometimes, Lemon wondered whether de Luca had been losing his touch at that point, hyped up on his own self-importance, chuffed with himself for creating more revenue with the sex parties.

Lemon had been entrusted with the task of finding the women. Oleksiy and Bohuslava from Ukraine had evaded him so far, and he'd reported back to de Luca that they must have had help getting out of London. For now, he had to keep an eye out, but he'd been relieved of the mission being one of his main jobs. Good, because trawling around London, a fucking big place, had taken a lot of time and had Capo questioning where he disappeared to.

Round the back of the house, Lemon cursed at his phone vibrating in his pocket. He hid in the shadows, close to the nearest outer wall, to read it in case it was de Luca, calling the last hit off.

"Fucking hell," he whispered.

He didn't need this shit at the minute.

VANGA: SORRY I HAVEN'T CHECKED IN UNTIL NOW. I'VE BEEN A BIT BUSY. SHE'S IN SOUTHEND. HOLED UP IN A CHALET. THE KID IS WITH HER. SHE WENT TO THE PIER, THEN RETURNED TO THE CHALET. THE LIGHTS HAVE JUST GONE OFF. WHAT DO YOU RECKON IS GOING ON? JUST A HOLIDAY? OR HAS SHE BEEN SENT THERE SO SHE'S OUT OF THE WAY FOR SOME REASON?

LEMON: FUCK KNOWS. NOW BOG OFF. YOU JUST WOKE ME UP.

It bothered him, though. Becky *must* have got a loan off the twins for her to be in Southend, which was better than her turning to prostitution, but it galled him that she'd got herself out of the hole he'd purposely put her in. He'd wanted her to suffer, to struggle without him, to realise the error of her nagging ways and beg for him to go back to her. Which he wouldn't, but seeing her pleading would have boosted his ego, satisfied him when he told her he wouldn't touch her again, even with a ten-foot bargepole. It seemed she'd moved on, then, if she'd stopped nipping round to his mum's and asking where he was, hinting she had no money. She was resourceful, he'd give her that, something he'd have expected at the start of their relationship, but he'd dragged her down, dimmed her light, snuffed out her self-confidence, and by the time he'd left, she was damn near broken.

The anger surging inside him prompted him to message Vanga.

LEMON: PAY HER A VISIT.

VANGA: WHAT?

LEMON: COVER YOUR FACE AND BREAK IN. SCARE HER A BIT. TELL HER SHE'S BEING FOLLOWED AND SHE NEEDS TO WATCH HER BACK, THAT THE SPARROWS THINK SHE COULD BE A LIABILITY. TELL HER TO KEEP HER MOUTH SHUT AND BE A GOOD GIRL.

VANGA: WHAT HAVE YOU BLOODY TOLD HER? FUCKING HELL, CAPO WILL GO MENTAL IF YOU'VE LET HER IN ON WHAT WE'RE UP TO.

LEMON: KEEP YOUR MOUTH SHUT ON THAT AND JUST DO AS I SAY.

VANGA: YOU'RE NOT THE BOSS.

LEMON: NOPE, BUT I'LL KILL YOU AS SOON AS LOOK AT YOU IF YOU DON'T DO WHAT I WANT.

VANGA: FUCKING NORA, KEEP YOUR WIG ON. WHAT DO I DO AFTER I SCARE HER?

LEMON: USE YOUR LOAF.

VANGA: WHATEVER.

Lemon pocketed his phone and moved along the back of the house. Lights ablaze in an office drew him closer, and he peered in at Mr Johnson sitting at a desk, the radiance from his computer screen illuminating his face. Lemon tapped on the window and slapped his back against the wall. Waited for the count of sixty. Slowly inched his face round so he used one eye to look inside again.

Johnson, if he'd heard the knock, had clearly deemed it nothing and had returned to whatever he'd been reading.

Lemon knocked again. Plastered himself to the wall. Waited. Checked the room.

Johnson wasn't there.

Lemon studied the exits—a single door down the other end, and French doors in the middle. Which one would the man poke his head out of, if he even did that? Or would he just phone the police?

Quickly, Lemon moved towards the French doors. A key turning in the lock sounded too far away to be where he was, so he scooted along to the single door. Steadied his breathing. Took his gun out and held it by his side. He leant his right shoulder on the house.

The door inched open, and through his goggles, Lemon made out half a nose, an eye, and one side of a mouth, all in a green hue. Heavy breathing indicated Johnson was afraid—and most likely without any hired help on hand if he was the one doing the investigating. Lemon already new Johnson didn't have a partner anymore—what wife would put up with her husband being a pervert unless she was one herself? And who in their right mind would allow him to have a refugee locked up in on one of the rooms? Or maybe she was in the cellar here. This was a big old house and was bound to have one.

Lemon scuffed his foot on the ground to create noise. It was so dark out now, he doubted Johnson could see him in his black getup, and being in the countryside helped to shroud the place in impenetrable shadows.

"Who's there?" Johnson asked.

Lemon scuffed again.

"I'm calling the police." Johnson remained by the door.

Lemon raised his gun. Aimed. From this angle, the bullet would enter the eye and come out through the side of the head, maybe skimming past the edge of the brain and not doing that much damage. Lemon had pride and didn't want to have to shoot the man twice. He was known as One-Shot Wonder in The Network and didn't want his reputation tarnished. So he walked forward, kicked the door so Johnson stepped back in shock, and smiled.

"Early morning call, sir. Move back slowly, hands up."

"What on earth *is* this?" Johnson obeyed, despite his question. "I have money in the safe. A watch, a Rolex. You can have it all."

Lemon followed him inside, seeing him perfectly clearly with his goggles on. "What we want is the woman you bought and for you to explain yourself."

"Eh?" Johnson darted his gaze around. "Explain myself for what? Woman? I don't know anything about a bloody woman. And who is *we*?"

"You know who *we* is, and the woman is called Zuzanna Majewski, otherwise known as Whore. That's what you call her, isn't it?"

Johnson sidled towards an internal doorway. "Please, whatever I've done, I can explain."

"No, I'll do that for you. You and a few others have been meeting up with a view to grassing the boss up to the police tomorrow. Giving names, telling on The Network, likely because you're afraid of the heat, of being found out and losing your women. You want everyone caught, but think about it: they might talk, hand your names over, so you'll be in the shit anyway. Prison isn't for the likes of you, is it. You couldn't handle being fucked up the arse on the daily. What you've done is against the rules—no corroborating with other Users, because that's what you are in the contract, a User. Deary me, what a mess you're in." He paused. "Sit on the floor, your back against the wall."

Johnson scrabbled to do his bidding, and it amused Lemon to watch a distinguished man reduced to doing as he was told with nothing he could do about it. There was a certain power here, Johnson relinquishing it, Lemon hogging it all to himself. Some men thought they were above all that, especially pricks like this who had money, but when it came down to the wire and it was obvious their lives were at stake, they all pissed their pants and turned into gibbering wrecks.

"All those in your 'boys' club' have been eliminated," Lemon said. "It's just you left."

"Please," Johnson blubbered, a sob catching in his throat. "Please, I'll do anything…"

"What you'll do is stay sitting the fuck down and shut up." Lemon knelt beside him. Placed the business end of the gun to the bloke's temple. "Night-night."

The headlights behind Lemon finally concerned him. He was the first to admit he had a big ego, and earlier, when he'd clocked being followed to all of the other locations, the cars continuing on whenever he'd turned into the streets, he'd been smug, thinking it was nothing to worry about, or at a stretch, de Luca checking up on him. Now, though… This vehicle had come close enough that he established the fact it was the same make as one of the previous cars that had been behind him. It worried him for a moment, until he convinced himself he was being stupid, acting not like Minion-66 but Lemon, being rattled by coincidences.

The two sides of himself had got muddled lately. Deep down, he'd always been like Minion-66, strong, fearless, and adept at doing his Network job, but switching to the Lemon people knew, the personality they all expected of him, the one he'd adopted to fit in at school and in life afterwards, to cover for his true feelings, it sometimes took a while to shake it off. Especially since he'd joined the Sparrows. He reckoned it was much like police officers dealt with when going deep undercover. Becoming someone else so much that by the time they finished the job and returned to their usual lives, slivers of the person they'd become had stayed behind.

He forced himself into his Minion mind-set. To test the driver, he drove until he got into Janine's neighbourhood then swerved onto a street that had houses on one side and a row of fast-food shops interspersed with pubs on the other. Although it was past midnight, people milled or staggered about, depending on how drunk they were, and several pockets of crowds stood eating from peach-coloured polystyrene food trays. Of course, the person in the car behind could be on their way here to collect some food rather than use Uber Eats; they might not be following him at all.

He snatched his night-vision goggles and balaclava off and threw them on the passenger seat. Parked and got out, heading for Shish King kebab house. Inside, he ordered a doner, all the salad, garlic mayo, and waited by the window, out of the way of other customers in the queue. The tail car wasn't out there, but it didn't mean the driver hadn't parked farther down, and with no means of identifying them, Lemon wouldn't have a clue if they walked in here now and ordered a burger and chips.

He paid for his food and took it back to the SUV, then drove away, his eye on the rearview. No one followed. Until they did, but it was too far back for him to check if it was the same car. He parked in Roland Avenue where Janine now lived, but the pursuing vehicle didn't come along. Telling himself he was just being paranoid, he ate his kebab with the plastic fork provided, still watching the rearview every so often in case the driver had got out of the car to watch him in person.

Nothing.

Belly full, he drove farther along the street and parked two doors down from Janine's. Light shone in the hallway, so he guessed she was still up, as she hadn't had it on at this time of night when he'd staked her gaff out before. He decided he had time for a little kip so set his phone alarm to wake him in a couple of hours. Two o'clock would be just the right time to break in and collect her.

Pleased with his night's work so far, he folded his arms and closed his eyes, dreaming of how he'd kill Dipsy.

Ichabod messaged the twins.

ICHABOD: HE'S OUTSIDE JANINE'S.

GG: WHERE ARE YOU?

ICHABOD: STANDING IN SOMEONE'S FRONT GARDEN. HE'S GONE TO SLEEP, SO MAYBE HE'S JUST STAKING HER PLACE OUT. SEEMS THE NETWORK DO HAVE A BEEF WITH HER.

GG: WE'LL SORT IT.

ICHABOD: HOW?

GG: YOU'LL SEE.

Chapter Ten

In bed, Janine scrolled through the message string on her burner again, crapping herself. If she rang the DCI about this, it could be one more nail in her coffin. If her boss was involved with The Network, it would look like she was still poking her nose into their business, and if they'd decided she wasn't to be bumped off, this could nudge them into changing their minds. But women had been moved from the homes of affluent men, the 'owners' of said women dead. She now knew the location of the house down the end of a track in the woods. What was she supposed to do with that information? She couldn't keep it quiet, couldn't leave the refugees to suffer, yet at the same time, she didn't want to implicate herself.

Fuck the time, she messaged the twins.

JANINE: BEEN THINKING. SOMEONE IS GOING TO HAVE TO INFORM THE POLICE, BECAUSE I CAN'T RISK IT. GIVE THEM THE NAMES OF THE MEN, SAY THEY'RE DEAD, AND PASS ON THE LOCATION TO WHAT'S OBVIOUSLY THE NEW REFUGEE HOUSE.

She switched her phone off so she didn't see the reply. Knowing George, he'd give her some excuse why he couldn't do the dirty work. Well, he bloody could. The pair of them had numerous burner phones on hand, God knew how many SIMs they could throw away, and it didn't take much to disguise a voice.

She stuck her mobile on the cabinet beside her and rolled onto her side, listening out for anyone breaking in, which she'd done ever since she'd come to bed. The new alarm would go off, but still, what if she couldn't get past an intruder? By the sounds of it, the man who did The Network's killing was a stealthy bastard well used to nipping inside houses. You only had to look at what had gone on tonight to know she'd be shit out of luck if he decided to come to her place. And it was Lemon, of all people. She'd swear blind he didn't have it in him, but he'd obviously been playing a role which he presented to the world, when in reality, he was a devious little fucker.

Four men, four shots to the head, then others had come for the women. It was a slick operation. She'd known that already, but for them all to move like ghosts and not do anything to alert the neighbours… Well executed.

Pardon the fucking pun.

She lifted her head and punched the pillow, then settled down again. If she slept it would be a miracle. She could have taken a sedative but had worried she'd sleep through anyone coming inside. Telling Colin her worries earlier, plus the twins informing her of tonight's bollocks, had brought her fears roaring back to the surface, and she'd gone to bed with the jitters. Maybe she'd be okay tomorrow. Maybe, because The Network hadn't touched her so far, they wouldn't bother at all.

If Lemon's out on the prowl again, though, it doesn't bode well for me.

What if she was right and they'd been biding their time, waiting for the heat to die down after Mallard's death? Four executions in one night spelled trouble. A third copper being killed would certainly raise more than a few eyebrows. The division had already caught enough flak from the public for Sykes and Mallard being murdered, so another copper, a woman at that, would have people even more up in arms.

She imagined the pain of being shot in the head. Or would it be so quick she wouldn't feel anything? She was guilty of dishing out the platitude 'It would have been sudden, they wouldn't have suffered' to many a grieving person. But what if that was a lie? What if it was the worst pain imaginable, and while it might only last a second, it could feel like hours?

She shuddered. Didn't want to die. She had so much more to do in life, not only in her legal job but with the twins. They'd grown on her, even though she pushed the boundaries and snapped at them from time to time. She recalled her behaviour when she'd first started working for them, how George, especially, had got a cob on

118

because she'd sounded too big for her boots. She hadn't liked taking orders, seeing as she was the one to dole them out at work, and although she'd been happy to take their money, she'd resented having to work for them. She hadn't had a choice in the matter. They'd picked her, and she'd agreed to do what they wanted. If she hadn't, they'd said they'd make her life difficult.

George had asked her to tone her attitude down, but that was how she was, *who* she was, and gradually, they'd got used to her sniping and seemed to have accepted it, much as she'd accepted George coming off as an arrogant prick every now and then. It was obvious she was just a crabby cow and didn't mean any offence. Besides, it wouldn't do them any harm to realise she couldn't drop everything for them, which they'd expected to begin with. Greg was in her corner there, reminding George that she straddled two camps and couldn't always run and do their bidding immediately. Leaving a crime scene not long after she'd arrived would look suspicious, so she'd taken to wandering off with the excuse she needed a moment to process it, then spoke to the twins on the phone or via messages.

It appeased them, and she maintained her cover.

The thought of dying and them bringing in a new copper brought on a surge of jealousy. It was *her* job to put herself on the line for them with regards to the police and any investigations they were involved in, not anyone else's.

A tear escaped. Odd. She didn't cry easily, not these days, but this shit had really got to her. Forced her to face up to her own mortality.

She wouldn't live forever. She wasn't indispensable.

A sobering thought.

A knock at her door had her stifling a scream and biting the side of her fist. Shit, was it Lemon? She got out of bed, heart hammering. Still unfamiliar with her new surroundings, she went over the house layout in her mind, reminding herself of where each room was and the furniture in them. She slipped her shoes on in case she had to make a run for it and tied the laces as she stared at her closed bedroom door. Another knock, and her hands shook. She stood, going to the window to look outside, remaining half behind the pink crushed-velvet curtain. A tall, burly man stood on her doorstep, his mouth obscured by a thick dark beard, his hair unruly curls. A holdall sat by his feet.

Has he got a gun in there? Fuck. Fuck!

He glanced up, lifted his thumb, then jerked it at her front door in a gesture that said, "Well, let me in, then!"

Would she fuck.

She grabbed her burner off the bedside cabinet and switched it back on. A couple of messages bleeped through.

GG: In light of tonight's bullshit, I'm sending Cameron round to look after you — no arguments. Tell people he's your new boyfriend or something if it raises questions.

GG: Fuck, Greg's just told me off for not giving you a description. Big bastard, black beard and hair. If you get close, as in you hit it off — come on, you could do with a shag, couldn't you, might make you less tetchy — I'm warning you, he's got the hairiest armpits I've ever seen. It's like he's got a puppy in a headlock.

She laughed, couldn't help herself, then scowled at George suggesting she'd be so unprofessional as to have a fumble with a hired bodyguard. And it had to be George, only he'd mention someone's armpits.

She returned to the window and opened it. Stuck her face out. Whisper-shouted, "What's your name?"

"Cameron."

"Who sent you?"

He glanced either side at her neighbours' houses. "You know it's best I don't say that out loud. Ring them, double-check, but if you want this bodyguard lark being done on the quiet, you're not doing a very good job. We're going to attract attention soon enough."

She checked the street, panicking.

"Hurry up, love, I need a cuppa and I've got work to do."

Work to do?

She took a picture of him and sent it to the twins.

JANINE: IS THAT HIM?

GG: YEAH.

Satisfied, she took her phone downstairs with her, disabled the alarm, and opened the door. She stepped back to allow him inside, locked up, then switched the hallway light on. He dropped the holdall on the floor.

"Oh." She gawped.

Despite the hairy caveman look, he was a bit of all right. His eyes, hazel, had her catching her breath like she starred in a ruddy romance.

Get a fucking grip, you twat.

She stalked off towards the kitchen, annoyed with herself, switching the lights on beneath the wall cabinets, snatching the kettle to fill it. She sensed his presence behind her, the hairs on her neck prickling. She examined that reaction, asking herself it was the wrong kind of response—that her warning bells were jangling. No, it was the attraction to him that had set it off.

Shit.

"I'll familiarise myself with the layout of the house, if you don't mind."

She put the kettle on its base. "If I don't mind? Like I have any choice."

"You don't, but I thought I'd be polite. It costs nothing to be nice."

She turned to face him, the kettle rumbling. "Somehow, I doubt you're nice, not with what you'd be expected to do for the twins."

"There is that, but that's a role I play. I'm not a bastard all the time."

Like Lemon? He's two people. So was Denny. Maybe everyone has different personas for different scenarios. I know I bloody do.

Cameron stared at her for too long, then walked out.

"Tea or coffee?" she called after him, flustered.

"Tea, please. Two sugars, seeing as you've implied I'm not sweet enough."

His footsteps banged on the stairs, and she thanked herself for buying a detached property. All right, it wasn't a grand affair; she hadn't been able to get too big of a mortgage otherwise questions would have been asked by her colleagues as to how she'd afforded such a gaff. She couldn't tell any nosy parkers she got paid more than her police wage from the twins. Still, she didn't allow any workmates into her personal space, and she wouldn't let any neighbours here know what she did for a living, so with the stash of money she'd saved from George and Greg, she planned to have a conservatory added.

She made the tea and carried the two cups to the table in the dining area. She sat, pondering her attraction to Cameron and how, in the past, she'd vowed never to have any kind of meaningful relationship again so had avoided men like the plague.

Cameron came back with her dressing gown. "Thought you might want to cover up."

Too late, she cottoned on that she'd opened the door in bed shorts and a skimpy, transparent cami top. "Um, thanks." Cheeks flaming —*what the fuck is* wrong *with me?* —she took it off him and put it on.

"I'll need the alarm code, your number plate, and your burner, personal, and work numbers." He sat and drew his tea towards him.

"Right." She gave him what he'd asked for, then put his number in the burner for now. She'd add it to her personal phone later. "So what's the deal? You're shadowing me?"

"Yep. When you get home from work of an evening, I'll come in through the back so anyone watching the street won't see me. I'm to stay here overnight until this crap is sorted. Oh, and I've got cameras to fit. One in each room."

She balked at that. "Even the bedroom and bathroom?"

"Yep. Shy, are you?"

"No, but I don't fancy anyone watching me undress or take a shit, thanks."

"Outside the bathroom, then, so I can see who goes in."

"And the bedroom?"

"I'll position it to the right by the window, so you can get dressed either in the bathroom or by the wardrobes on the left. I'm not fucking about here, Janine. I've been told to shadow you, to make sure you're safe, so any modesty will have to go out of the window until we're sure The Network isn't coming after you."

She gritted her teeth. Didn't like being dictated to. "Fine." Then she admitted she was relieved. She could sleep now, knowing he was here, and during the day at work, she'd feel safer with him tailing her. "You will be careful when I'm out at crime scenes, won't you. I mean, there will be loads of coppers about, and I can't be doing with them asking you why you're loitering around. They might think you're a suspect, coming back to view his handiwork."

He sighed. "I've been doing this for a long time."

She inhaled. Released it. "Right. Then I suppose I just have to trust you, don't I."

"Something like that." He sipped his tea. "Nicest cup I've had in a long time."

Weirdly, she felt chuffed about that. "Don't let your missus hear you say that. She might get offended."

"I don't have one." He eyed her over the rim of the cup.

Jesus Christ, she was in trouble here.

No fucking around with the hired help.

"What about a fella?" she asked.

"Nope."

She couldn't hide her smile.

Chapter Eleven

George sat in the living room alone. Greg had gone to bed, grumbling about being up so late when they had shit to do tomorrow, although George thought it would be a better idea to get hold of Lemon now in case he attempted to hurt Janine. Lemon was clearly in a killing mood, and the fact he'd murdered people earlier was a bloody big indication that he was involved with

The Network. If he wasn't, why had men come to collect women and take them to that house? Could there be another reason behind those actions? Were the women the men's wives, kidnapped, and other family members would be asked to pay a ransom now the blokes were dead?

It didn't matter, because George had gone out in the car to make the call to the police, away from their house, parking down a shady side street. He'd used his Ruffian voice, a Scottish accent, and informed the bird on the other end of the line that women had been abducted, giving the names and addresses of the four men, plus the house in the woods, hinting it was something to do with The Network.

Will had followed the kidnappers to their homes, and George had passed on those locations, too. By now, whoever had been in that house would probably be in cells down the nick, the women taken to hospital to be checked over, and the abductors also sitting in a cell, crapping their kecks.

The least Janine had to do with the organisation, the better it would be for her. He understood her paranoia, and she'd been right all along to be wary. With Lemon currently napping outside her house, it proved she had plenty to be worried about. Cameron was there now, though, and he'd been told not to tell her Lemon was watching. When Lemon died, served up on a platter with indications in place that he was with The Network, she might be called out to the scene. Not knowing he'd obviously been stalking her would be the best way to go. She wouldn't have to hide those emotions regarding it, on top of the ones she probably already experienced — hatred towards a previously ghost-like man who must be the assassin used to kill Mallard, not to mention the others who'd been executed so they couldn't open their mouths.

How was she coping, knowing it was Lemon? George had heard of him prior to this, but as a twat who had a gob on him and wasn't anyone to worry about. Since Becky had let them know he was worth being on their radar, George had been jotting down notes so they could do another sweep of the estate to remind residents that if they saw something dodgy going on, it was their duty to report it to him and Greg.

How many more big sweeps would they have to do before people finally got the fucking gist, though? Weren't they being scary enough? Did they have to, yet again, return to acting like the thugs they'd been when they'd first started working for Ron Cardigan? Did people need to see others being hurt before they'd *listen*?

Maybe kneecapping and Cheshire smiles were no longer enough.

Or maybe people thought George was going soft, keep topping up people's leccy meters and giving them money when they hit a tight spot. In future, he'd tell those he helped to keep their mouths shut about it. While he enjoyed being a saviour, he'd forgo the praise if it meant people went back to being proper shit scared of him.

The grief counselling he and Greg had been getting from their therapist, Vic Collins, had worked wonders, but it had played a big part in George honouring their mother by doing good deeds in her place. The public knowledge of such acts *had* to stop, and if there were other gangs fucking about like the Sparrows, George needed to know about it. This was major egg on his and Greg's faces, and he didn't like being undermined, nor did he enjoy the thought of people laughing behind their backs at the Sparrows pulling the wool over their eyes.

Trusted men in the firm had been sent out to watch other Sparrow members, although one of them, who went by the name of Baba Vanga, hadn't been located. He wasn't at home, and when one firm member, in disguise as a priest, had enquired about him at the local pub, people had claimed they hadn't seen him since the day before.

Had Lemon eliminated him before Ichabod had begun his surveillance? If so, why?

One of the others, Dipsy, had been selling on The Judas Estate all evening from the confines of his Ford Focus. At least it meant he wasn't selling on Cardigan, and a quick courtesy call to Prince Judas had revealed the leader knew all about the sales because he was taking a cut. That estate wasn't George's concern, Cardigan and Moon were. No reports had come in about drugs being dealt on Moon, so he hadn't had to get hold of his good friend to warn him, but the twins' estate was another matter. Three Sparrows had prime spots, all of them being watched, and they'd be taken to the warehouse once they returned to their homes.

At the last check-in, Capo, the Sparrow boss, sat in his living room glued to the telly with a woman by his side, the curtains open so they were easily observed. Seemed he dished out the orders and let everyone else do the dirty work.

Well, the fucking lot of them would feel the pain of George's tools before long. They had some explaining to do, and he was in just the right mood to ask questions.

Chapter Twelve

*B*ecky had been hanging around with Daksh ever since Mr Tomlinson's suspension, bound to him by their mutual experience. A meeting with Mrs Guttenberg and their parents had revealed that the inquiry into his behaviour, taking their statements into account and him finally admitting to it all, begrudgingly, had led to his termination of employment. Charlene had come back to school but had *thankfully stopped saying things to Becky and Daksh, but she still threw them filthy looks. Mr Tomlinson now worked in Sainsbury's, so Becky's mum avoided going there as she wasn't sure if she could be her usual polite self if she saw him.*

Becky, her head full of the film they'd just seen at the Odeon, linked her arm with Daksh's as they navigated the dark streets, heading towards home. Fifteen now, they were allowed out until ten on a Saturday, providing they were together, and only if they were going somewhere like the cinema, bowling, or at each other's houses, their mums and dads present at all times.

Both sets of parents feared reprisals from the Tomlinson affair, worried that Charlene and her friends would want to get their own back, waiting for a few months so suspicion didn't fall on them if something happened. With racially motivated knife crime so prevalent, and with the story of Stephen Lawrence forever embedded in their minds, they walked quickly, Becky glancing left and right to catch sight of anyone who might be a threat.

What must it be like to walk without fear?

She didn't know, and being female, she had an extra level of anxiety on top.

They came to the part of their journey that gave two options—keep going through the two lit streets they had left or cut through the park.

"Keep going," Daksh said. "I'm not walking through there."

"I was just going to say the same thing."

They continued on, and farther down the street, just after the phone box, they drew near to an alley between houses that also led to the park. Becky glanced down it; halfway along, the light from the streetlamps didn't penetrate, and the rest of the alley was in complete darkness, the slit of the park at the end presenting as darker shapes against the moonlit shroud—the height of the slide, the side poles of a set of swings.

She shivered and tugged Daksh's arm for him to move faster. Wished she'd taken Dad up on his offer of coming to pick them up from the cinema instead of stupidly walking to Daksh's and his father dropping her home from there. She was surprised Daksh had been allowed to walk. His strict parents normally said no.

A call for help startled her, and she spun round, twirling Daksh with her, and stared at the alley. "Did you hear that?"

"Yeah. We should phone the police."

"Help…" It sounded like a woman.

"Oh God," Becky said. "What if she's been hurt on her way through the park and collapsed in the alley?"

"I don't know, but we shouldn't go down there."

"I'm bleeding!" the woman wailed.

Becky couldn't stand by and do nothing. She dithered, though, switching between going down the alley and knocking on someone's door. Daksh peered along at the alleyway, which was six houses away now, then diverted his gaze to the phone box.

"I don't know what to do," he whispered.

"Phone for an ambulance. We'll go and see if we can help her."

"Please," the woman called. "Oh God, please…"

They ran to the phone box, Daksh going inside, Becky propping the door open, her breathing heavy. He stabbed at the number nine of the keypad then listened. "Police. Ambulance. Someone's hurt in the alley in Lion Road. She's bleeding."

He slammed the receiver down, and they made their way along the pavement, fear sending Becky's legs wobbly. She gripped Daksh's hand and stopped at the end of the alley. Whoever was in there was in the darkest portion. She glanced at the house to the left and let go of Daksh and went up the path, feeling too young, too afraid to deal with this. An adult could take charge.

She knocked, but no one answered.

"I think...I think I'm dying," the woman said.

Shit. Becky's instinct kicked in, and she rushed into the alley, then slowed, mindful in the dark section that she couldn't see the person and might accidentally hurt her more if she bumped into her. Footsteps from behind, and Daksh slipped his hand in hers.

"Where are you?" Becky called into the void.

"Here..."

They took a couple more steps. Daksh grunted, and his hand slipped from hers, weird scuffling sounds echoing.

Panicked, Becky turned in the blackness in search of her friend. "Daksh?"

"Run!" he said, his voice strangled.

"Where are you?" Becky's chest hurt it was that tight.

"Just run!"

"I can't leave you!"

Another voice joined the conversation. "Don't you dare walk away, Sutton."

Mr Tomlinson? What was he *doing here? Oh God, had he hurt the woman?*

Another grunt, then the sounds of another scuffle. Someone bashed into Becky, and a familiar hand, fingers linking with hers, gave her a measure of comfort. Tugged by Daksh, she legged it to the other end of the alley, towards the park, guessing he led them that way because Mr Tomlinson blocked the other entrance. She stumbled, her feet going from pounding the pavement to hitting the spongy grass, and she caught sight of Daksh beside her.

"Oh my God! What happened in there?" she asked, running, running, running.

"He…he had his hand around my throat."

Thuds behind them had Becky glancing over her shoulder. "Shit, he's coming! What about that poor woman?"

"I don't think there is a woman. He must have followed us from the cinema then went into the park down the road, going into the alley from the other side."

"Would he have had time?"

"If he ran. Get moving. Faster!"

Halfway through the park, past the play area, Daksh tripped over and went sprawling. Becky stopped to help him up. Mr Tomlinson barrelled into her, knocking her off her feet. She hit the ground hard and rolled onto her front, pushing up on her knees. The ex-teacher gripped her hair and hauled her onto her feet, dragging her towards the trees that bordered the area. An ice pick of fear stabbed at her all over, her blood going cold, her legs growing heavy from the shock and terror.

"Leave her alone!" Daksh shouted. "The police are coming."

"Shut your mouth, Paki."

Mr Tomlinson shoved Becky through an opening between trees; the 'den', the locals kids called it, a space inside where little children went or teens hung out to smoke. He thrust her up against a tree and held something to her throat. She couldn't see what it was, the darkness had taken over again, but it had to be a blade, it was too cool for it not to be.

"Get off her," Daksh said.

"He's got a knife," Becky screeched.

The blade disappeared, Mr Tomlinson's hand taking its place. He gripped her neck tight, and she struggled to breathe.

"You lost me my job, you fucking little cow. I got a caution off the police for racial slurs. My daughter did, too. Do you know what you've done? How you've ruined my life?"

He let out an oof and jolted against her. Daksh must have hit him. Something landed softly in the mulchy leaves. Had Mr Tomlinson dropped the knife? His weight grew less intense, and his hand left her neck. She gasped in fresh air, tears falling, her throat sore not only from his squeeze but the large lump of emotion that lodged there. She pushed off the tree and scoured the dark for Daksh, seeing nothing but the bare skeletons of trees and specks of lightened sky in the high boughs from the moon.

"Daksh? Where are you?"

"Get off me!" he said.

A series of noises that meant another scuffle was going on. The rustle of leaves. The grunts and heavy breathing. It seemed to go on forever yet at the same time lasted only seconds.

"Shit. Oh God," Daksh said, his words fracturing the air. "Oh God!"

Desperate to know what was going on, Becky staggered towards the den opening and turned to face where she'd come from in case she could see things better from there. As with the alley, the farther reaches were too dark, but Daksh stood in enough moonlight near the entrance for her to spot his silhouette. He had his back to her, and he stared ahead, then came rushing out, a hand to his mouth. Was he going to be sick?

"What's going on?" Becky asked, panic adding a quiver to her words. "What happened?"

"I s-stabbed h-him."

The unexpected admission floored her. She swayed, her head going dizzy, and backed away from the scene

142

of the crime. Oh God, had anyone seen them going down the alley? Could they see them now from the rear windows of the houses? Where were the police and the ambulance? Shouldn't they be here by now? What if they got caught...got the blame, as if Daksh had planned to kill that horrible man?

"Where's...where's the knife?" she whispered.

"I dropped it."

"Is he...dead?"

"I don't know, I can't see in there." He sobbed. "This will bring shame on my family..."

He'd taught her a lot about his culture, how his parents dissected every choice he made, and if it didn't conform to their ideals, he would bring shame on them and their community. They policed every part of his life, expecting him to do better than anyone else, gently prodding him with their advice if he didn't achieve their high standards, forcing him to try harder. He wasn't allowed a girlfriend, one would be chosen for him when they felt the time was right—he was only allowed to hang around with Becky because they knew her mum and dad from the racism group and didn't feel there was anything like love growing between them. He'd explained it was just their way and that in effect, Indian parents loved their children so much they

143

just wanted what was best for them and it blinkered them to anything other than what they deemed correct.

For him to be involved in this… He couldn't be. It would ruin his chances of becoming a solicitor, his parents had chosen that profession for him, and if the truth of this got out, the family might be cast out of their circle, other family members and their community turning their backs on them.

Daksh didn't deserve that. Even though what he'd done would be classed as self-defence, Becky was all too aware that his skin colour might play a big part in him being sent down anyway. The police around here had already been accused of being institutionally racist, time and again. Could they take the risk that the truth would be heard?

No.

Despite her need to always do the right and legal thing, she chose the other path so her friend wouldn't be ostracised, so the rest of his life wasn't ruined. That was the right thing to do, too, wasn't it? She owed him. He'd backed her up when she'd gone to tell Mrs Guttenberg about Tomlinson.

"Go and get it," she said.

"What?"

"We'll leave it somewhere. Hurry up, the police will be here in a minute."

144

He vanished into the den, returning with the weapon, and together, they ran down another alley at the back of the park and into Bleacher Avenue. Under the light of a streetlamp, she checked him over. If he had blood on his clothing, she couldn't see it—his coat and trousers were black. But his hand...it had something on it. And, oh God, there would be fingerprints on the knife handle.

She checked the nearby houses for anyone watching, then had a thought. If they hurried, they could make it to the public toilets that stayed open all night on Church Lane. It would mean explaining why they were so late getting to Daksh's house, but they'd gone over time anyway by going into that alley so already needed to come up with an excuse.

At the toilets, Becky pushed the main door open using her elbow. Daksh washed the knife then his hands. He used paper towels from the dispenser to wipe the weapon all over, then the tap he'd touched. Becky flushed the towel down the toilet and cleaned the loo handle with her sleeve. They left the knife in the sink and went back out into the street.

"What if he isn't dead?" Daksh whispered. "He could tell on us. It would look like I hurt him because of what he did at school. And I used the phone. My fingerprints will be on the buttons and handset."

"You haven't been in trouble with the police before, and so long as you never are in the future, no one will know it was you." She imagined the ambulance and the police had turned up at the scene by now. "We have to get to yours. Say we were late because of the crowd at the cinema, and we'll say that next time we'll have a lift home. We'll make out we walked down Felix Street instead of the one by the alley. No one would think you'd stab anyone, you're too kind. How did you get hold of the knife?"

"He dropped it. When he got off you, he came at me. Touched…touched me, like he did in the classroom."

"Touched you?"

"Down there."

Revolted, she said, "Why didn't you say so to Mrs Guttenberg?"

"It would bring shame."

Becky frowned, quickening her pace. "What a filthy bastard he is. You'll need to wash your coat. Can you do that without your mum wanting to know why?"

"No."

"Bring it round my house tomorrow. Mum and Dad will be at the group."

"So will mine, but my mother will know if I use the machine. She knows everything."

146

Becky couldn't imagine living under such strict scrutiny, but Daksh had assured her he was used to it, it was all he knew, and it was better than not being cared for at all. He respected his parents more than anyone else she knew.

"We'll sort it, all right? Now shh, we're by your house. Act normal."

It would be tough, but they had to do it. Tomorrow, they could discuss everything and get their stories straighter.

For now, they had to lie through their teeth.

Chapter Thirteen

Becky, startled awake by something, sat bolt upright in bed and listened. Her breathing ramped up, ragged, and she glanced over at Noah's shape in the cot. Carefully, she manoeuvred so she could reach over and touch his tummy to make sure he was really there, that it wasn't a puddle of blankets she'd seen. The steady rise and fall of his chest gave her relief, but

149

something had woken her, and she had to find out what it was.

Staying in a strange place didn't help, and the unfamiliarity had her footsteps faltering. The bedroom was a different layout to at home, the door at the bottom of the bed rather than at the side, but she navigated the darkness and crept into the living area, her gaze drawn to the full-panelled glass door to her right in the dining/kitchen area. A person's silhouette stood outside, all in black, their hand reaching inside a hole in the broken glass to fiddle with the key in the lock.

Why the fuck had she left it there?

She turned and ran back to the bedroom, grabbing Noah, then her phone, and rushed back out into the living room, a sob brewing. A quick glance at the rear door told her to get the fuck out of there—he'd opened it and stepped inside. At the front door, she scrabbled with the Yale, her heart going too fast, fear sending her knees weak. She had to make it outside, had to save Noah.

She wrenched the door open just as he fisted the back of her nightie and hauled her in reverse towards him, her back slamming against his chest. She opened her mouth to scream, but a hand slapped over it. Desperate, she kicked back, but her foot met with air. He reached forward and pushed the door closed, then dragged her to the sofa and threw her on it. She clutched the sleeping Noah tightly, her throat pitter-pattering with her rapid pulse, and willed her baby to remain asleep.

"Don't scream, don't speak," he said.

She stared up at him, too petrified to move, yet a nagging voice in the back of her head said to try and run for it again, to get Noah to safety. Go via the back door, getting glass in her feet be damned.

"I've followed you all the way from London," he said.

She didn't recognise his voice, nor could she make out any features other than a paler shade of skin inside the eye circles of a balaclava, fleshy lips poking through the hole lower down.

"I've been told to tell you to keep your mouth shut about the Sparrows, but I'm beginning to wonder whether your little visit with The Brothers was more than them just helping you out with money. You went to Yiannis' shop, didn't you, stocked up, so I know the twins paid you. What for, though, eh? Information? Or was that your first payment for a job as a slapper on Debbie's Corner?" He paused. "I'll let you speak now so you can answer me, but I'm warning you, if you scream, I'll kill that fucking kid of yours."

He must have been following her all day. She'd had the feeling of being watched, hadn't she, when she'd stood on the steel landing outside Debbie's door. Why was she being followed *now*, though? Lemon had told her about the Sparrows ages ago—or had she been watched ever since he'd left her? This was just like him to arrange something like that. Someone keeping an eye on her and reporting back.

"I g-got a loan," she said, cursing herself for stuttering. How could she not when he stood in front of her, all in black, holding something down by his side? "My baby's father doesn't pay me anything for him."

The man sighed.

She babbled on. "We moved to that house together, it's more rent than I can afford on my own, otherwise I'd never have gone there. I'm on maternity pay. It's hard. George gave me two grand."

"So you decided to have a little holiday, did you?"

"Yes. I needed to get away. Rethink my life."

"What do you know about the Sparrows?"

She could lie, say she didn't know anything, but she sensed this was a test. "That they sell drugs and fuck people up. Sometimes, they hand over the gear then follow the buyer to steal it back off them to resell it. The boss has guns he loans out to people for a thousand quid a time. That's it." She hoped she sounded unbothered, that having the information didn't mean anything to her and she wouldn't do anything with it. Then the idea of another form of test hit her. What if he'd asked her what she knew to see if she was willing to blab? Which she just had. *Fuck*.

"You know nothing else about what we're doing?"

"No." So it was okay for her to have revealed what she knew if he was a Sparrow. Which one was he, though?

"You were with the twins for a fair while. Are you *sure* you only asked for a loan?"

"Yes! They're mates with Debbie and stayed for lunch; I was asked to stay, too. I didn't say a word about the Sparrows. I'm not stupid. Lemon would probably kill me, and if he didn't, his mother would be round my house like a shot, having a go if I dobbed her precious son in. It isn't worth the hassle. I just want to live in peace with my son. Look, you're wasting your time here. I've got nothing I want to say to anyone about your lot."

"How do you know I'm with the Sparrows?"

"You said 'we'. And you're here, aren't you? Honestly, just go away and leave me alone." She came off as tired, not scared, but inside, she was bricking it.

"You don't get to tell me what to do. I'm the one with the gun, not you." He lifted it, waved it around.

It wasn't difficult to see its shape in the dark, but it could be a fake for all she knew. Still, she wasn't about to risk it. "I promise you, the Sparrows' secret is safe with me."

"Are you going to work for Debbie?"

She laughed in an attempt to appear calm. "I might have to once the loan runs out."

"Then you won't mind giving me a sample, will you."

"*What*?" Fear bounded up her windpipe and closed her throat.

"You heard me. Put that kid down." He jerked the gun. "Do it!"

She stalled for time, to think. Oh God, why couldn't she *think*? "But he might wake up and roll off the sofa!"

"Put him in the bedroom."

Slowly, she got up, going through her mind to remember where certain things were in the chalet. Beside the bedroom door stood an occasional table with a tall iron giraffe on top. If she held the head with both hands and swung the base at him, it could do a bit of damage, but first she had to put Noah in the cot.

In the bedroom, she lowered him into it, placed her phone next to him, and left the blankets to one side for ease of grabbing him and the mobile after she'd hit the man.

"I don't want to do anything in the same room as him, so can we go back to the sofa?" How odd to be saying that, as if she was okay with what he had planned. Even odder that she sounded fine, as if she'd given consent. But if she had to play a role to save her son, she'd let this bastard paw her as much as he liked.

"Fine, just hurry up."

She turned to find him in the doorway. "Will you let me past, then?"

He stepped back into the living room, watching her exit, then spun to walk towards the sofa. She snatched the giraffe up and held it high. She ran at him, bringing it down on the back of his head, a horrible thud denoting it had hit his skull. He let out a roar of pain and stumbled away, then spun and aimed the gun at her.

"Get on that sofa." He reached up to touch the back of his head. "You fucking broke my nut." He lowered his hand and stared at the blood on it, which looked black in the dark. "Shit, I've got a headache. When Lemon and Capo find out what you've done, you're dead meat."

She imagined his eyes shone with malice, soldering the truth of his words into her mind so she was under no illusion that he'd meant what he'd said. She sat.

He took a pair of cuffs from his pocket and threw them at her. "Put those on."

Shaking, she did as she was told but left them loose enough so that later, she had a good chance of getting them off. "What do you want me to do, lie down?"

He shook his head, his eyes scrunching in a wince. "I'm not doing it to you yet. Like I said, headache." He laughed. "Isn't that what all you women say?"

"Your head…you should ring for an ambulance."

"And that's going to go down well for me, isn't it. 'Why did she hit you, sir?' 'Oh, I just broke in and threatened to rape her, nothing to worry about.' Are you off your tree?"

She tried to catch an inflection in his voice so she could work out who he was, but the voice was deeper than anyone she'd met before, and it had an exaggerated East End accent. Whoever he was, he was definitely from the Sparrows.

He paced. Agitated. "Look, cards on the table. I like you, okay? I don't agree with how Lemon's been treating you and the kid. He told me to come here. I didn't want to, but he threatened me."

"We've got something in common, then."

"My position is difficult. I have to do shit or I look weak if I don't. Got to prove myself."

"What, for some silly gang?"

He stopped pacing and stared at her. That 'silly gang' is my life. It's going to get me somewhere one day."

"Not if The Brothers find out."

"Listen to me, you. We've been operating for a while now, right under their noses, and they don't have a clue."

"You need to be careful. They'll find out in the end, and they'll be after the lot of you. The rules are simple: fuck them over and you're dead. If I were you, I'd get out now while you can."

"But you're not me, are you? You haven't lived my life, haven't been told you'll amount to nothing. Haven't had people telling you you're worthless."

"Haven't I?"

He tutted. "Christ, I should let you go."

She acted nonchalant, although hope blared inside her. If he was thinking that way, he had a conscience. "So do it, then. It's one thing running round selling drugs and whatever, but holding me and my son hostage? Think about the prison sentence for that. And bear in mind the twins will be sending someone to my house to collect the first loan repayment this time next week. If I'm not there to pay up, they'll want to know why. They'll poke into it. So if you've been told to kill me or whatever, you'll be caught in the end. You know what they're like. Dogs with bones."

"Shit." He sat on the armchair opposite, gun held lazily over the side. He groaned and touched his head again. "This has gone further than it should have." He'd let his guard down a little; a touch of another voice had seeped through.

"Do I know you?"

He jerked, shocked. "What are you on about?"

"Your voice. I thought…"

"Nah, nah, you don't know me."

If the light was on, she'd be able to see his lips, his eyes. She could maybe work it out then, but the darkness was his best friend, shielding his identity. Come the morning, though, if he was still here, she'd get a good look.

"Who are you trying to convince, me or you?" she said.

"Shut up, all right? Just shut up."

She pushed some more. "What did Lemon tell you to do to me? Did he say it was okay to rape me? To cuff me?"

"Be quiet, I need to think."

She glanced at the bedroom door behind him. Her baby lay beyond it, innocent. He didn't deserve to be caught up in this, no more than she did. All she'd done was think Lemon loved her, she'd believed his promises, and she'd ended up in this mess.

Would she ever get the chance to make something of herself? Would George's offer of her having her dream job even happen?

When the man lifted the gun and pointed it at her, she had a feeling it wouldn't.

Vanga had gone down the wrong path. Why did shit never go the way he planned? Lemon had told him to use his loaf, but he'd backed himself into a corner he didn't know how to get out of. When he'd said Becky could give him a sample, he hadn't even meant it. He'd been high on adrenaline, power, and it had slipped out of his mouth. He knew why. He'd fancied her for ages, wished she was his girlfriend, not Lemon's.

When Vanga had first met her, she'd been so different. Alive, full of vitamins as his nan would say, eyes all sparkly, and she'd laughed a lot back then. It hadn't taken long for Lemon to do a number on her, like he'd done to the woman who'd come before Becky. Lemon had a thing about teaching the 'little women' in his life how to behave, and it had sickened Vanga every time.

They'd grown up together, the only men in the Sparrows who'd known each other before joining up. Best mates, that's what he thought they were, but lately, it was clear Lemon used Vanga as a lackey, someone to boss around after wheedling his way into being Capo's right-hand man, a position Vanga thought *he'd* have. Lemon had come to the gang later than everyone else, and only because Vanga had vouched for him.

I shouldn't have asked Capo if he could join.

That was a thought. Maybe Vanga ought to let Capo know that Lemon was dishing out orders. Then he remembered the texts.

YOU'RE NOT THE BOSS.

NOPE, BUT I'LL KILL YOU AS SOON AS LOOK AT YOU IF YOU DON'T DO WHAT I WANT.

That was true, the killing bit. There had been times over the years when a weird side to Lemon had come out, as if a blob of darkness lived in him and it sometimes showed itself. He talked about popping a cap in people to shut them up, but Vanga had taken it that it was just shit talk, a drunk man bigging it up. When he'd got that text, though, he'd sat up and taken notice. Lemon was so into being a Sparrow that killing was probably his next step. Vanga had overheard Lemon and Capo whispering about Dipsy, saying he needed teaching a lesson. Vanga reckoned the pair of them had decided to take it up a notch, to be a higher level of gang.

I don't want to be involved in that sort of crap.

Drugs and duffing people up were about his limit, yet here he was, with a gun aimed at Becky, saying nasty stuff to her so she didn't twig it was him. He lowered it. Guessed she was shit scared, even though she'd sounded calm. She'd be worrying about Noah in the other room.

"I'm not going to hurt you or the kid," he said and got up, ashamed he'd said he would rape her and kill Noah. That wasn't who he was. "Stay there. I need to lock the back door." Walking in reverse, he watched her for signs of movement. Hoped she didn't dart to the front door, because that would mean he'd have to shoot her, and it would also mean she didn't love Noah more than herself if she was willing to leave him behind.

She stayed in place, and he crunched over the glass and turned the key, drawing the curtains across. The hole in the glass could be a problem if someone from another chalet heard them talking come the morning.

What are you on about, the morning? Get the fuck out of here and go home.

He took his phone from his pocket and messaged Lemon. He needed guidance out of this mess. But what if Lemon told him to do the nasty and kill her and the kid?

He didn't think he could go through with it.

Chapter Fourteen

A t the sound of the alarm, Lemon woke and checked his personal phone. Vanga had got hold of him.

Vanga: Things have gone a bit tits up, mate. I scared her like you said, and she reckons she won't say anything about us lot, but she hit me with something, and it's broken a bit of my

FUCKING SKULL. I'VE CUFFED HER, BUT WHAT DO I DO NOW?

Lemon gritted his teeth. If this was Vanga using his loaf, he dreaded to think what he'd do if he *really* put his mind to something. It had been a simple order, to basically go and scare her, but by the sounds of it, things had gone too far.

LEMON: WHAT A DICKHEAD! I THOUGHT I COULD TRUST YOU TO SHIT HER UP THEN GO HOME. WHY DID YOU EVEN HAVE CUFFS ON YOU, FOR FUCK'S SAKE?

VANGA: DUNNO. SHOULD I LEAVE NOW?

LEMON: WHAT, AND GIVE HER A CHANCE TO RING THE FUCKING POLICE AS SOON AS YOU DRIVE OFF? IF THEY CATCH UP WITH YOU…

VANGA: I'VE GOT A GUN. IF I'M STOPPED AND THEY FIND IT…

Lemon blew out a stream of air. Vanga was a bastard waste of space. He sorted through his mind for some way out of this so Vanga could get back to London without being seen.

LEMON: GOOGLE BACKROADS HOME. YOU NEED TO STAY AWAY FROM CAMERAS. DID YOU USE YOUR OWN CAR?

VANGA: WELL, YEAH. YOU DIDN'T SAY I HAD TO NICK ONE AND PUT ON DODGY PLATES.

LEMON: CHRIST! SO IF SHE RINGS THE POLICE, AND THEY POKE INTO THINGS, THEY'RE GOING TO SPOT YOUR NUMBER PLATE. YOU'LL BE QUESTIONED AS TO WHY YOU WENT TO SOUTHEND AND WHAT FOR. WHAT ARE YOU GOING TO SAY?

VANGA: DUNNO. HAVEN'T THOUGHT THAT FAR AHEAD.

LEMON: THEN THINK, BECAUSE YOU NEED A SOLID ALIBI. YOU'RE GOING TO HAVE TO SHUT HER UP.

VANGA: HOW? PERSUADE HER NOT TO TELL THE PIGS?

LEMON: THAT OR KILL HER.

VANGA: I'M NOT DOING THAT!

LEMON: THEN YOU'D BETTER GET ON WITH THREATENING HER. SHE'S WEAK NOW, SHE'LL DO WHATEVER YOU SAY, I MADE SURE OF THAT. TELL HER THE SPARROWS WILL BE WATCHING HER FROM NOW ON, AND IF SHE PUTS A FOOT WRONG, SHE'S DEAD. WHAT DID SHE SAY ABOUT THE BROTHERS, OR DIDN'T YOU EVEN BOTHER TO ASK?

VANGA: SHE GOT A LOAN OFF THEM, SO IT'S ALL GOOD.

LEMON: SHE COULD JUST BE SAYING THAT. PUSH HER ON IT AGAIN. KEEP ASKING HER ABOUT THEM, SEE IF SHE SLIPS UP. YOU NEED TO BE OUT OF THERE

BEFORE THE SUN COMES UP, THOUGH. DOES SHE KNOW IT'S YOU?

VANGA: NAH, I PUT ON A VOICE.

LEMON: THAT'S SOMETHING, THEN.

VANGA: SO YOU WANT ME TO SCARE HER SOME MORE SO I CAN GET AWAY?

LEMON: YES, THICKO. NOW FUCK OFF AND SORT YOUR MESS OUT.

Lemon turned his sound alerts off and slipped his personal phone in his pocket. When he'd first woken, he'd been right in Minion-66 mode, but now he'd segued back into Lemon because Vanga was incompetent and had given him something else to worry about. He leant his head back, closed his eyes, and channelled his inner 66, dredging up all the feelings he used to have when he'd been 66 permanently. A stone-cold killer. Someone who didn't take any shit.

The old emotions returned, his heart hardening, his mind clear of the crap Vanga had created. A quick glance around the street, and he was satisfied no one watched him. Mind you, if he thought there was a risk, he wouldn't have gone to sleep. His concerns earlier about being followed had proved to be a waste of time.

He put his goggles on over his balaclava, checked his gun was in the holster, and left the car, leaving it unlocked for the ease of a quick getaway once he'd nabbed Janine. He scanned the street, again seeing nothing, and walked up her short garden path. He anticipated packing boxes all over the place so prepared himself to scoot around them if she hadn't put everything away yet from her recent move. Using the services of one of the other Minions, he'd acquired the blueprints for these houses a couple of days ago and memorised the layout, so unless the previous owners had knocked down walls, he knew where he was going.

At the back, he steadied his breathing in the small paved garden, not a patch of grass in sight. Trees and shrubs bordered the edges, growing tight against the six-foot wooden fencing. The homes behind it didn't have lights on, and neither did those either side of Janine's, which also stood in darkness apart from a faint blueish glow poking round the edges of the curtains in the room directly above. A night light on the landing, perhaps, filtering into the back bedroom, or maybe she used it as an office and she was working late.

Whatever, it was safe enough.

He took a lock pick from his pocket and inserted it into the door that led into the kitchen/diner. A couple of fiddles, then he turned the handle down.

No alarm went off; he hadn't seen a box on the house and had guessed correctly there wasn't any security installed, although some alarms didn't have deterrent boxes these days.

Shrugging, lock in his pocket, gun in hand, he went inside.

On the monitor in the back bedroom, the screen facing away from the window so only a dim glow crept outside around the curtains, Cameron watched Lemon enter the kitchen. Ichabod had let him know when Lemon had got out of the SUV and approached the house. Janine was in bed, snoring—the rumbles came through the dividing wall—and Cameron stood as Lemon walked through into the hallway.

He continued staring at the screen until the target embarked on climbing the stairs. Cameron threw his jacket over the monitor to douse the light then stood by the wall in the bedroom, the door open, his gun ready. Lemon had made it to the landing and crept along towards Janine's bedroom. Cameron followed. Went right up behind him.

Lemon reached out and gripped the handle.

In three swift moves, Cameron held the back of Lemon's black jacket, had his gun pressed to the man's temple, and his face close to his ear. "I wouldn't bother, mate."

Almost too fast for Cameron to process, Lemon jerked his body to the right and lunged forward, his jacket sleeves sliding off, then he turned, taking something from the region of his side and bringing it up to eye level. Cameron dropped the jacket and nutted Lemon in the face before he could use the weapon, then kneed him in the bollocks. Lemon bent over with an *oof*, staggering sideways, heading for the little spare room at the front. Cameron pursued, shooting him in the arse, the silencer deadening the sound. Lemon thumped into the closed door, sagging to his knees. Cameron snatched the weapon out of his hand, a gun, tossing it behind him. He dragged the goggles and balaclava off, throwing them on the floor, gripping Lemon's hair and drawing his head back.

Cameron shoved the end of the gun in his mouth. "Like I said, I wouldn't bother, mate. Now get up, nice and slow. Me and you are going downstairs. One shitty move in the wrong direction, and I'll blow your fucking brains out. On your feet."

Still holding his hair, Cameron marched him along the landing. The snoring had stopped, and Cameron didn't wait for Janine to appear—she had to have heard the gunshot, despite it being dulled. He threw Lemon down the stairs, the bloke going arse over tit the whole way down, then chased after him, not giving him enough time to get up and escape. A kick to the face soon sorted any notions Lemon had of running, and Cameron hauled him upright and steered him into the kitchen. He flicked the light on and guided him to the table.

"Sit."

Lemon did that but eyed the exit.

"You won't get away." Cameron smiled at the sight of Ichabod in a balaclava appearing at the open back door.

"Ye've been caught, ye fuckin' eejit, so sit there and do as ye told." Ichabod entered, his gun trained on Lemon. He took his balaclava off. "Ye've been a busy boy, haven't ye. Running around London killin' perverts. While that's commendable, it isn't right that women have been removed from the houses and taken tae some other place. I'd have thought ye'd have already been informed the police have rescued them, but it seems your boss isn't the kind tae let ye in on somethin' like that, unless he doesn't know yet."

Lemon's face twitched. "Fuck you."

"No thanks." Ichabod sat opposite. Casual. Unruffled. "Listen tae me. I'm tired from gallivantin' around after ye, so bear in mind I might get a bit trigger happy if ye give me any gyp."

"I've already shot him in the arse," Cameron said.

Ichabod laughed. "And busted his nose by the look of it. Nothin' more than he deserves."

Janine walked into the kitchen, her dressing gown tied tight, and stared at Lemon who had blood dripping from his nose. So she'd been right, The Network *were* after shutting her up.

"Did the twins know he was here?" she directed at Ichabod.

"Hmm. I've been followin' him all night."

She folded her arms and glared at Cameron, indignance rearing up inside her. "And no one thought to tell *me* about it? I mean, it's only my *life* that was in danger."

"George felt it best you didn't know," Cameron said. "So you didn't worry and got some sleep."

Her anger softened a bit. She looked at Lemon. "Call yourself a killer? How the *fuck* have you let someone overpower you? I'd have thought The Network would have chosen a better assassin than that."

The barb had hit home: Lemon winced.

"He's been tae busy runnin' around with the Sparrows, got himself out of practise." Ichabod drummed his fingertips on the table.

Lemon's eyes closed slightly, a tell that told Janine all she needed to know.

"You got in with the Sparrows as a cover, didn't you?" she asked, not expecting an answer.

Lemon snorted. "You're going to be so fucked over this. The boss is already after you. Do you think that by killing me, which is what I suspect is going to happen, he'll back off? You'll be getting rid of the best asset he has in London. He won't be pleased. There will be someone else after me, someone who won't be allowed to make a mistake."

Ichabod leant back and smirked. "I had a little look in that SUV out there before I came in here. You're slippin'. That phone you left in the glove box hasn't got a PIN code. I know your boss' number—he was in the Merc, wasn't he, he's in *London*. The twins will find him by the Merc number plate if it isn't fake. Lucky for us, The Brothers know a couple of people who monitor the council CCTV. It won't be long before the data of the Merc's journeys has been sent through. We'll find him."

If The Brothers didn't find de Luca through the Merc and Janine had to poke into the phone number, de Luca might find out she'd used the police database to track it, and she'd be fucked. Then again, she was fucked anyway, wasn't she?

There was already a hit out on her, so even with Cameron trying to keep her safe, she could still get murdered.

Sod it, I'll have to use someone else's login details to get the info.

She hated doing that. She'd done it before on a computer used by several people in a private office, had watched their keystrokes as they'd logged in, then used their codes to look up various cars and names for the twins, nothing that would raise red flags. It would have to be in the morning, though, and only if no one else was in that office. If she turned up at work now, in the middle of the night, it would lift a few eyebrows.

Fuck it. She *had* to help George and Greg find de Luca, because she was certain someone on the refugee team was bent and passed him information. Why else had he come to London? He thought it was safe now, that the investigation had stalled. He'd been given the green light to enter the country.

She sighed. "You're going to be tortured, you know that, don't you."

Lemon shrugged. "All good things come to an end. I had a decent run."

She gawped at him. Was that all he could say? Why wasn't he bothered about being hurt? Killed? What kind of man was he that he seemed to have accepted his fate? Or did he have an ace up his sleeve? Was someone outside in a car now, sent to shadow Lemon? Were they waiting for him to emerge, either with or without her, and see where he went next?

"The street," she said.

"Nobody's out there," Ichabod said.

Her shoulders slumped in relief.

Lemon smiled at her. "Scared you, didn't I."

She'd never admit it to him. Never.

Lemon's arrogance hadn't allowed him to contemplate being caught and interrogated, but now he came to think about it, it bothered him quite a bit that the twins had engineered all this and had caught him. Unless he could get away from them, this was the end of the line. Annoyance barged into him that he wouldn't be able to kill Dipsy now if he couldn't escape. Weird, how his two sides warred for prominence now. Lemon, the bloke who thought he was the

177

up-and-coming gangster, and Minion-66, the man no one ever saw until it was too late.

Where had 66 gone? How had Lemon allowed that part of himself to disappear to the degree that he hadn't been thinking straight?

Because de Luca told me to become someone else for a while, and by the time I got back into it, trying to track the Polish bitches and keeping tabs on Janine, I'd gone rusty.

It burned him that the Irishman had been right.

Lemon knew he should have left Janine until tomorrow. He'd said that to de Luca. Or had he just thought it? No, de Luca had said Lemon might have time after he'd killed the men, planting the seed in his head, and like a fool, he'd let his ego take over, agreeing that yes, he had time. The big bearded fella must have come here while Lemon was off murdering, and it was obvious now that Ichabod had been tailing him to every kill scene.

That bloody car I clocked.

As for the police knowing about it… De Luca was going to go off his nut when he found out the new refugee house had been discovered, but that wasn't down to Lemon. The blokes who'd taken the women must have fucked up somewhere down the line, so they'd be the ones to cop it.

He didn't like asking questions in this sort of situation because it showed the opposition what you didn't know, but he *wanted* to know so he could appease himself, could find out if *he'd* been the one to muff up.

"How do you know where the women went?"

The Irishman chuffed out a laugh. "Someone else waited outside the houses and watched what was goin' on. The abductors must be a bit on the thick side if they didn't see headlights behind them. Mind ye, the same could be said for ye. I was close to ye a couple of times, yet still ye went ahead with it. Did ye think ye were untouchable?"

That was about the size of it. Lemon cursed being with the Sparrows. If he wasn't, he wouldn't have made such a lame mistake. He'd have let de Luca know the mission needed to be aborted and tried again another day. He'd allowed his ego to rule, something de Luca had warned him about, saying it would get him into trouble one day.

So why did he keep me on if he thought I was a liability?

Because I'm the best at what I do.

Was the best.

"What happens now?" he asked, ignoring the man's question.

"Ye'll be goin' tae the warehouse, fella. I think I'll come along and watch for the craic."

Chapter Fifteen

De Luca rested in his plush hotel bed and stared at the ceiling, here as another alias he'd created for his first trip back to London in a while. Amedeo Bianchi. A lamp on the cabinet next to him cast the room in a buttery radiance, and he enjoyed the benefit of the air-conditioning being on just enough to take the mugginess out of the air. That was the trouble with British summers, too humid, and the weather was so unpredictable. Earlier, it had been a little chilly, yet the afternoon had warmed up, the evening turning into a hot one. He preferred his latest location where he'd settled, Antigua. It was warm year-round. Winters there were about twenty-four degrees, the height of summer in the thirties.

He loved his new base, where he was safe and known as Paolo Campagna, a businessman who worked from his expensive home and didn't draw attention to himself. He'd be a fool to adopt the life he'd led in Italy as de Luca, everyone's hero, a man who'd helped the poor as a cover for what he really did. They'd revered him there, as they had his papà before he'd died, and de Luca had to admit, he missed the adoration. He'd also missed being in the thick of it with The Network, and the months of lying low and reducing operations had been galling, boring.

No new women had been persuaded to leave their homeland to start afresh in the various locations around the world with the promise of a nice place to live and a job, money in their pockets. The refugee house being discovered in the East End, not to mention the buried bodies of women who hadn't been up to scratch, had meant he'd had to close down bringing in any new recruits and tell everyone to live unobtrusive lives so they weren't discovered.

He used to have three people in the London police force who helped him, who were a part of The Network, but now only one remained. Sykes had been killed by God only knew who, and de Luca had ordered for Mallard to be expunged because he'd proved to be incompetent, admitting to Janine Sheldon under pressure that he was involved in it up to his neck since Sykes had brought him into the fold.

Now there was Janine to sort, a job he'd purposely left until now so the heat died down. Minion-66 hadn't made contact since he'd reported in after each of the men's murders, which said he hadn't collected Janine yet or killed that person called Dipsy. Maybe he was waiting until the witching hour to do those jobs. No matter, de Luca trusted him. 66 had never let him down before.

He closed his eyes. He'd come to London to oversee the new captive house and talk to the person who he'd chosen to take over from Denny after he'd disappeared without a word. The man, Minion-15, had been a recruiter in the past, someone who'd gone overseas and picked out women ripe for stealing. 15 knew how careful they had to be now, and he was an asset, much better than Denny, so once he messaged to say the four women had been recaptured and were at the house, de Luca would go there in the Merc, another set of false plates put on, and inspect the goods to see how they'd fared while living with the murdered men.

He hoped they'd been mistreated. That they had bruises and had been taught their place. Unlike his mother in the early days, who'd been a refugee and had wheedled her way into Papà's affections, tricking him into thinking she was the love of his life, when in reality, she'd used him in order to elevate herself from prostitute to someone who'd swanned around the house dishing out orders.

Her behaviour was the reason why de Luca didn't trust women. They should all know their place, all do as they were told, and if they had a strong will and a mind of their own, he wanted to crush their spirit.

That was why it would be so delightful to hear about how Lemon had abducted Janine, tortured her, taking her down a peg or twenty. That woman was a pest, a bloodhound after the scent, and she'd signed her own death warrant by poking into his business.

Chapter Sixteen

*B*ecky hadn't slept well since the incident in the den. Her dreams had been filled with horrors, her watching the stabbing in the daylight instead of being blinded by the dark, seeing every movement, every time Daksh struggled and Tomlinson got the upper hand. She viewed their faces—Daksh's terror-filled, Tomlinson's wreathed in spite—and it churned her stomach when the blade entered the bastard's body.

Where, she didn't know, neither did Daksh, but her mind filled the blanks in various ways: a slice to the neck, a pierce to the heart, a raw wound in his thigh, the blade slashing the fabric of his trousers. She always woke sweating, her chest filled with panicked dragonflies, their wings beating in time with her throbbing heart, her eyes sore from where she must have cried in her sleep.

A week had passed, and no police officer had come knocking on the door. She wasn't sure if that was a blessing or not. The anticipation of it happening wreaked havoc with her mind, but it was just as bad as it not happening. How could she go through life pretending this hadn't occurred, like she'd suggested to Daksh they should? She would, there was no way she'd open her mouth about it, getting him into trouble, but it would be a big burden to carry to her grave. It had already changed her so much, so God knew how different she'd be in the years to come.

She'd read somewhere that trauma shaped you, and you could either learn from it and still flourish or dwell on it and become bitter. The bitter had crept in a couple of days ago. She'd been ashamed of herself for thinking badly of Daksh. It had only been a fleeting thought, but the fact it had appeared in her head meant she must harbour some resentment towards him, deep down.

He'd had no choice but to defend himself, but why did it have to happen? Why had Tomlinson followed them, which he must have? Why had fate decided that was a good idea?

Of course, she'd squashed that thought as soon as the guilt of it had stabbed at her with its pecking beak, but it was natural, wasn't it, to wish things had gone the other way? To sit there and imagine an alternative scenario, where they'd managed to run away to the opposite alley, Mr Tomlinson not catching up to them. Then they'd only have had the threat of him trying to waylay them again at a later date, rather than this God-awful fear that they'd be caught and tried for murder.

Conversely, she was glad he had *been stabbed so he* couldn't *come after them again. What sort of person was she to be glad someone had died? She wrestled with that daily.*

As it was Saturday, they were meant to be going bowling. She didn't feel like it, Daksh had said the same at school yesterday, but if they didn't go, his parents would question him as to why, and they didn't need that kind of attention. They had to live like nothing had happened.

Charlene hadn't been at school all week. News had spread, in the papers and through gossip, that Mr

Tomlinson had been attacked in the park. The local rag said whoever had killed him had lied when phoning the police, saying a woman had been attacked. That untruth had to stay between Becky and Daksh; people had to believe whatever they wanted to, because if they opened their mouths and admitted what had really happened, Daksh, and Becky by association, would be in big trouble.

That Mr Tomlinson had pretended to be a woman proved how sick in the head he was, how devious, and how he'd done whatever it had taken to lure them into the darkness. She couldn't comprehend hating someone so much that strangling them, putting a blade to their neck, and touching them inappropriately was the way to go.

It was such a monumental thing for her to cope with, all of it. That day last week, they'd been like any other kids, enjoying a night out, but it had ended in tragic circumstances. Mr Tomlinson had been unconscious when he'd been carted into the ambulance and had died on the way to the hospital. Daksh had nicked an artery, and the horrible man had bled out in the den, the emergency services held up elsewhere, getting to him too late for a blood transfusion to save him. As the police had at first tried to find the distressed woman, vital minutes had passed by the time they'd found him in the den. He'd apparently fallen after being stabbed and cracked his head open on a tree stump.

The knife had been discovered in the toilets early the next morning by the cleaner. The patches of sleeplessness between nightmares had been plagued by fear that Daksh hadn't wiped all of his fingerprints off the surfaces he'd touched, and that hers would be found on the flush handle despite her cleaning it. They lived in a perpetual state of terror, of being found out, and the last five days at school had been awful, neither of them eating much during lunch. To only have each other to talk to was the load they'd have to carry. Becky longed to tell Mum, but she'd tell Auntie Shelia, who'd then tell her colleagues, and it would all go tits up.

Silence was their only friend.

Daksh's coat had been washed and dried just in time. Becky had not long taken it out of the tumble dryer when her parents had arrived home from the meeting. They'd been trying to play Monopoly at the dining table, although their concentration was shot, the game paused every now and then to go over and over their alibi, and that was where her mum and dad had found them, seemingly innocent teenagers enjoying a Sunday afternoon, fake smiles in place, *their shaking hands hidden beneath the edge of the table.*

Tonight, Daksh's father had dropped them off at the bowling alley with the promise he'd be back to collect them at ten, pleased they'd chosen to heed his well-meaning advice and had been 'sensible' in taking the lift. He'd nodded at them in the rearview mirror, then went on to tell them that he'd ordered the meat for the meal he was cooking tomorrow. After another group meeting, the families were getting together. Mr Gupta planned to make curry, and Dad had opted to provide a Jamaican one, too, blending their cultures over a meal. Normally, Becky would be pleased, she loved the fact the families had bonded so well, but it meant too many eyes on them. Too many people who could ask, "You don't seem yourself lately. What's wrong?"

They tagged onto the queue in the café section of the bowling alley and ordered hot dogs and chips. They didn't speak, several ears were around, a few people from school. Becky carried their tray to the tables, and they ate, sipping Cokes and not talking much.

Then Daksh whispered, "I'm a killer."

Maybe it had finally dawned on him, like properly. He'd been watching the other kids, perhaps envying them their freedom from all things horrific.

"Don't," Becky said, and in an attempt to make up for that nasty thought she'd had last week, she added, "You couldn't help it. If he hadn't followed us, none of that would have happened."

"What do you think he was going to do with us if I hadn't...if it hadn't all gone wrong?"

She had no doubts about that and had gone over it a million times. "Killed me—he had his hand around my throat, remember. If you hadn't hit him, I reckon I'd be dead." She'd taken to putting a scarf on, grateful the cold weather meant it wasn't an unusual thing to do, but indoors it was trickier, so she'd worn her turtleneck jumper to death until the bruises had faded.

"I think he'd have raped me after strangling you," Daksh said, a frown furrowing.

"I don't know. And about that... It's confusing. He hated you, yet he..."

"I know. I can't get my head around it. If he hated me, how could he touch me down there?"

"Maybe he was fucked up," she said. "Like, he was mental in the head or something."

"I think it was a power thing. It didn't matter who I was, he just wanted to take control of me." Daksh glanced around at the other diners. They were too far away to pick up on anything, yet he still whispered, "Do you think we'll ever get caught?"

"Not unless someone can identify us." She shook her head. "It said in one of the reports that two people were spotted but it was too dark to see their faces."

"We're too dark, they mean."

"Hmm."

"And that bothers me. What if the police look into his past and see he was cautioned for racism? They'll know all about us reporting him and might put two and two together."

"They'd have done that by now, and we haven't been spoken to, so don't worry about it." Easier said than done. She'd already had the same thoughts herself—two people, too dark to see, was a polite way of saying the assailants were probably black. Daksh could be mistaken for being so. "Look, let's put this behind us. Tell ourselves it didn't even happen. If we keep acting off, not eating and stuff, someone's going to notice, especially your parents."

"They already have, so I've had to force myself to eat." He bit into his hot dog as if to prove the point.

"Right, let's try and enjoy ourselves tonight. It's going to be hard, but the more time that passes, the safer we'll be. I'll never grass you up, you know that, don't you?"

"Same."

They held hands. Best friends forever, locked in solidarity because of a man who'd harboured hatred in his heart.

She never wanted to meet anyone like Mr Tomlinson again.

Chapter Seventeen

The man hadn't spoken for ages after he'd messaged someone on his phone. Probably Lemon. Becky prayed Noah would sleep in come the morning. He did sometimes, providing no loud noises woke him up. As the holiday park was in a quiet location, set amongst the trees, unless the people in the chalets either side of her created a racket, it should be all right. The longer he was unaware of the masked stranger, the better Becky would feel. Later on, Noah wouldn't remember him even if he *did* see him, he was far too young, but she was conscious that the things going on in a child's life affected them as adults, even if incidents had long been forgotten. They shaped you, changed you, and she didn't want this to have bad connotations for her son. He could become afraid, the balaclava representing fear in his mind, fear Becky transferred to him in her tight hold, and if he saw one later in life, he could become upset.

For years, she'd coped with Mr Tomlinson's death, how it had changed her. How she always wanted to do the right thing yet had hidden such a big secret. Even now, she worried that a cold case police team would reopen the investigation and they'd be caught. Mind you, one of the newspaper reports, a month after the death, had suggested there *had* been a woman involved, that she'd been attacked and killed him in self-defence, going into hiding because she was too ashamed to admit what had happened. It seemed the police had lost interest, or hadn't had any leads, and the case had been filed away.

Still, even now, Becky invented scenarios where there was a knock at the door and coppers stood there. She'd be taken to a police station, questioned, and she'd be forced to reveal the truth, no matter that she'd vowed never to drop her friend in the shit.

She'd kept in contact with Daksh for a long time afterwards, but as the years had rolled by, he'd been so busy at uni, then starting his first job, that their contact had trickled to nothing. Their parents still got together at the meetings, and they'd continued their Sunday meals once a month, their bond stronger than ever.

How did Daksh feel as a solicitor, or maybe he was a barrister by now, defending people who'd killed? Did it bring back memories for him? She'd heard through Mum he was married and had moved to Sheffield to be near extended family, having two kids quickly, a third on the way. Becky, glad her mate had found happiness, couldn't help but envy him. He'd removed himself from London, loved his wife who had been chosen for him, and had seemingly put it all behind him.

That was an uncharitable thought. He was probably like her, their secret never far from his mind. He likely beat himself up every day. Had he stopped contacting Becky because she reminded him of what he'd done? Or was he just too busy? She hoped it was the latter.

Her surroundings forcing her out of her head, she swallowed tightly. Had the urge to check on Noah, see if he was breathing, but the man might think she was up to something. She glanced over at the baby monitor on the kitchen worktop, but the green light wasn't on. That was right, she'd switched it off when she'd gone to bed.

"Can I…um…can I turn the monitor on so I can hear if Noah wakes up?"

"Yeah, but no funny business. I'll be watching."

She got up and walked over slowly so he wasn't spooked by any sharp movements. She switched the monitor on, and a rustling sound came through where Noah had probably turned over, and she itched to go and see if he was okay. What if he'd snagged a blanket with his arm and it had gone over his face? She raised the volume and returned to the sofa, pushing her motherly instinct down.

"Why did you call him Noah anyway?" the bloke asked.

"It means 'rest, peace', and I want him to have a restful, peaceful life."

"Why?"

"Because parts of mine weren't like that, they were shit. I don't want my son to have to go through what I did."

"What's that then?"

"Racism." She wasn't prepared to go into it any deeper; she couldn't tell a stranger that her best friend was a killer. No matter how she tried to explain it, he wouldn't understand. He was white, couldn't possibly get it, how they'd been petrified of being arrested on the back of someone implying they'd been too dark to see in the night.

The man chuffed out a grunt. "He might go through shit anyway, or worse, because he's half black, half white."

She was well aware of that and intended to teach Noah both sides of his heritage so he could be proud of who he was. "I'll protect him."

"Didn't your parents protect you?"

"Yes, they stood by me when I had to grass a racist up, but they don't know about other stuff. If they did, they'd have my back." They would, too. They'd also be too afraid that Becky being black would mean she'd automatically be a

201

suspect, which would bring out their parental instincts to shield her from trouble.

"What happened?"

"I don't want to talk about it."

"Childhood is so crap. I didn't have much of one myself. We were always skint, and Lemon—"

He cleared his throat, maybe to get rid of the words lodged there that he hadn't said because they'd give her a clue as to who he was. The mention of 'childhood' and 'Lemon' in the same sentence gave her enough to go on. Whoever he was, he'd known Lemon for a long time. Lemon hadn't had many mates when she'd first met him, only Vanga and a bloke called Dave, and this man didn't sound like either of them.

"You knew him as a kid, then," she said.

"Nah, I was just going to say that Lemon taught me to go for what I want so when I have kids, they won't go hungry."

He'd either lied or she'd jumped the gun, desperate to put a name to the voice.

She wanted him to dislike Lemon, to see a side to him he might not know about. "I feel the same way, but unfortunately, with Lemon not contributing and me living in a house with a stupidly high rent, a house *he* pushed for us to live in, my child might well go hungry when I go back to work. There's the childcare costs, and I might end up being just as penniless as I am now by the time I've paid for it."

"You could get a Universal Credit top-up. What about your parents?"

"My mum and dad are getting their own lives back, so I don't want to push Noah onto them. They've already brought me up, given up so I didn't go without, so why should they do it all over again just because I chose a shit boyfriend?"

"How shit was he?"

"He's good at gaslighting. That should tell you all you need to know."

"You're not the same as when you first met him." Then he muttered, "Shit!"

He'd slipped up. So he *did* know her.

"How would you know?" she asked.

"Doesn't matter."

She shrugged, even though he might not be able to see it in the dark. "He broke me down, made me feel stupid, that I was worthless. I put up with it because I thought I loved him. All those nights when he stayed away from home, leaving me by myself, I got to thinking about how he was probably shagging someone else, and I realised I was worth more than being treated like shit. So I started a row, and that was when he told me about being with the Sparrows, like that justified his treatment of me. I questioned him every day after that, trying to get him to see hanging about with the Sparrows would get him in trouble, maybe even in the nick, and d'you know what he said?"

"No."

"That being in the nick was better than being with me. Then he packed his stuff and left. Ever since then, I've struggled—I even nicked nappies and bread from Yiannis, for God's sake. I couldn't ask Mum and Dad for more money. I'd already done it enough when Lemon lived there because he'd stopped contributing. I asked his mum for help, but if you know her, you won't be surprised that she basically told me to fuck off and implied Noah wasn't Lemon's."

"Jesus. Sorry you had to go through that."

"So that's why I got a loan from the twins. I had nowhere else to turn."

"What about your aunt, the copper?"

"What about her? Why should my aunt or uncle dip their hands in their pockets because I can't cope? It isn't their problem. So I'm moving out of that bloody house and going somewhere with lower rent. *If* you're not going to kill me, obviously. You could walk out of here now and I wouldn't say anything. Just so you know." She'd tell the twins, that was a given, but a little lie might get rid of him.

He remained silent.

"I'm not stupid," she said. "If I go round saying you broke in here and threatened me with rape and a gun, saying you'd kill my son, Lemon will come after me. I've got Noah to consider. Do you think I'd put him at risk?"

"No."

"So leave, then. Pretend this never happened." Those words took her right back to that terrible night.

He stood. "Look, it all went a bit wrong. I was supposed to come in here and warn you to keep your gob shut, that's all. I didn't even want to do it, but he said he'd kill me if I didn't."

"And you believe him?"

"Yeah. You must have seen is dark side."

She had, but she answered, "What do you mean?"

"I reckon he's killed before. He talks about offing people when he's pissed up."

Her skin went cold. "What?"

"You said he stayed away from home sometimes, yeah? Well, as far as I know, he didn't have another woman when he was with you, and he wouldn't have to stay anywhere on Sparrow business, so think about it, why *else* would he have to hide?"

"Who would he have killed, though?"

"I dunno." He sat again, leaning back, the gun and his hand resting on his stomach. "But I can't risk him turning on me."

"Was it him you were messaging?"

"Yeah."

"What did he tell you to do?"

"Make sure your story about The Brothers was true, tell you the Sparrows will fuck you up if you talk, and for me to get out before the sun comes up."

"You've done all but the last thing, so maybe you should do as he says and go now. I broke your skull—you need to go and see a doctor."

He touched his head. "Maybe."

Chapter Eighteen

Seven dead members of the Sparrows slumped on folding chairs in the warehouse, the usual coils of rope around their middles keeping them in place. George had got bored with their whining, and they hadn't offered up much info apart from the fact they sold drugs and Capo loaned guns out, so he'd shot them in the forehead. The septuplets, as George now thought of them, because they all had the same outfits on and with the hoods up appeared identical, had likely rued the day they'd joined the gang as soon as they'd been dragged out of their homes earlier. Hindsight, it was a terrible bitch, but it had come too late for them.

Blood spatter marred the ropes, and each man had wiggly dribbles of claret going from the gunshot wounds and down their faces, which had dripped onto their black hoodies. He'd walked round and inspected the backs of their heads after the last one had been dispatched, smiling at the state of them. Wounds so nasty they didn't look real, instead resembling makeup done on a horror film set. Blood and brain bits dirtied the floor, the force of the bullets so strong that some pink-grey bits had landed on the blade of his circular saw waiting patiently on the table. He'd trodden over the mess without a care, then returned to stand in front of the others.

Lemon, very much alive, sat on the original wooden torture chair at the end of the row—he had the most to be interrogated about so deserved the prime spot. George had killed the others starting at the left end, so each remaining man knew when their time would come. The other two, Capo and Dipsy, stared ahead at Greg sitting on the sofa playing *Call of Duty*, the gunshots and screams from the telly speakers adding a nice audio backdrop. Ichabod stood beside George, a hammer in hand. He and George had forensic suits on, and Ichabod was a man after George's own heart—he didn't bother with a face mask so must enjoy the feel of hot blood splashing his skin, too.

I knew there was a reason I liked that bloke.

"I hope you three will have more to say for yourselves than that lot." George indicated the septuplets with a jerk of his head. "From what I gathered, Capo, while you seem to think you're the big bad boss man, your dead colleagues reckon Lemon is someone to be worried about more than you. Is that right? I'm asking because Lemon's refusing to talk now, and you might give me the information I want." He bent and moved closer. "Between you and me, I think a bit of rack torture is in order for him, but all in good time."

George had been in the process of nodding off on the sofa at home when the call had come in that all the men had been collected from their homes and deposited at the warehouse. Capo's woman had been told to keep her mouth shut if she knew what was good for her, and she'd nodded her response, tears in her eyes. None of the men in the Cardigan firm had announced who'd sent them, so any pointing fingers would be aimed at fuck all.

He was wide awake now and ready to get into the swing of things. It seemed like forever since they'd spoken to Becky at Debbie's. So much had gone on. Greg wasn't too grumpy, he'd got a few hours' kip, so that was something. He'd opted to play his game so Ichabod could get a front-row seat and be George's wingman instead. The casino manager had chosen the hammer as his weapon of choice to 'kneecap the feckin' bastards if they so much as look at ye funny'.

Easing back to a standing position, George toyed with the cricket stump, slapping it on his gloved palm, enjoying the flinches from Capo and Dipsy. They might be wondering what damage the stump could do, but if they took note of the now brown bloodstains, they'd know it could hurt. George particularly liked ramming it into eye sockets. Whether he would today or not was anyone's guess. He wasn't angry enough to imagine the pleasure of gore—Mad George and Ruffian hadn't shown themselves yet, and the septuplets had brought on apathy in him, the feeling of this being same old, same old, people waffling on, speaking too fast in an attempt to be pardoned.

"So, Capo, what do you have to say for yourself?" he asked.

"For what?" Capo said.

Ah, there it was, a spark of anger inside George at his belligerence. Who the *fuck* did this bloke think he was? "As if you don't know. Weren't you *listening* when I interrogated your employees? I'll spell it out for you: selling drugs on Cardigan without permission. *And* not giving us a cut as protection money. You know how this works. If you want your business kept safe, you pay us so we can make sure no one touches you. Selling on Judas doesn't count. You have *Prince's* permission to do it there, but not here."

"I didn't realise," Capo said, going for a bullshit answer, one the septuplets had already disputed; they'd all said the same, that Capo had told them he'd already gained permission, so they thought they weren't doing anything wrong. "I thought you just had to ask any old leader and it was all right."

George laughed darkly. This bloke was taking him for a fucking mug. That spark of anger grew, and Mad George joined the conversation at last. *Took your fucking time, mate.* "Then you're the only one so far who claims to not know the order of play. How long have you lived here, my old son?"

"All my life."

"Then you *know* the rules. Let's refresh for those at the back who *can't fucking hear*," he shouted. "Each estate has its own leader—granted, Cardigan has two—and you can only operate on each estate on each leader's say-so. You don't just gad about doing what the fuck you like. How long have the Sparrows been a thing? I mean, we haven't heard of you until now, and I suppose you'd say that's because you're all shit-hot at working under the radar, but I reckon it's because you're a bunch of no-mark novices, which is why you didn't come to our attention sooner. No one contacted us and grassed you up because they didn't think you were worth bothering with. You're a joke, and everyone's been laughing behind your backs. We know—we checked."

The fact they hadn't been aware of the gang pissed George the fuck off, but he wouldn't let them know how much it had bothered him. Cardigan was a big area to cover, but they had no excuse—there were two of them running it. Mind you, the fact they were always together (unless George buggered off to become Ruffian), meant they had so much ground they didn't get to cover. That, and always having shit to sort out, their time was limited.

He nodded to himself, satisfied with that excuse. Justifying why the Sparrows had been able to operate undetected. Yes, he'd known of the members, thought they were just dickhead blokes like so many others were in London, but he hadn't for one minute thought they had enough brains between them to run down the shop for a packet of bog roll, let alone engage in gang life.

"You're wrong," Capo said. "People *are* scared of us. We've told them if they tell you about us, they're dead."

George's laughter barked out. "Really? Did you think they'd be more scared of you than they are of *us*?"

What if they are, though? What if we're losing our edge?

"They shit themselves," Capo said and puffed his chest out.

He believes his own hype. Am I guilty of doing the same?

George didn't like having parallels with people like this knob, and the anger inside him grew, spreading, heating his cheeks. "They obeyed a little prick like *you*? Fuck me sideways, what is the world coming to, eh? Let me think about this. Say I'm your average resident. I've got two men like me and Greg on one side, blokes who have no worries about chopping people into bits while they're still alive, and *you* on the other, a moron who'd get knocked over by a puff of fucking wind and wouldn't have the balls to cut into a steak let alone a body. Hmm, which one would I be more afraid of?"

"You don't have to be big and a bully to scare people," Capo said. "Words can be enough to scare them."

"Oh, they can. I'm good with my words." Yet despite that, George wasn't getting through to this man. Even with the septuplets dead, Capo still thought he was the man. *Change tack.* "By the

214

way, we've taken all the cash and drugs out of your house as backdated protection payments, not that you've got a business for us to protect anymore, and all those guns in your loft, well, they're ours now—until we drop them down the nick anonymously." He'd leave them in a secure location and give Janine the nod. "They're bound to have your fingerprints on them, and you've got a record, so I've been told, so when you go 'missing', everyone will know you loaned guns out to people who shouldn't be anywhere near them. Your name will be mud."

He had an idea to see whether Capo's ego was that big he'd be chuffed about the next statement or show some remorse. George detested children being killed, and if Capo was proud of what he'd played a part in, then George would know all he needed to: that Capo was only after money, and whatever happened in his quest to get it, he didn't care so long as his pockets got lined.

George needed to fuel his fire and brought the scene to mind, how it had gone down. A dark residential street, a kid called Jason walking home after being round his mate's house, a night of fun on the PlayStation. A pizza delivery, popcorn and Magnums for afters, Haribos to follow. Lads being lads, doing what boys did, hyped up on excitement and the sugar rush. Four doors from his house, someone coming up behind him, calling him a dickhead, giving a reason why Jason had been followed and had a gun pointed at him—a gun Capo had provided. The gunman—or gun*child*—Kaden, a known troublemaker. Hands up, *please don't hurt me*. A shot, footsteps, laughter with a whoop as an exclamation mark. Jason on the pavement, people coming out to see what had happened. His mother, running down the garden path, "No, no, no," coming out of her mouth. Kneeling. A scream. Blood, so much blood, and the last words before his final breath: "Thank you for my life, Ma."

George clamped his teeth, eyes stinging. What a way to go. What a fucking tragedy. He steeled himself to continue. "Take this for an example: a kid—who ended up killing another kid. That's what happened, wasn't it? The case on the news last week, a fifteen-year-old boy shooting a fourteen-year-old for no reason other than he gave him a filthy look. Does that sit well with you to know you had a hand in that? And where the *fuck* did that boy Kaden get the money from to borrow a gun off you?"

"What they do with the guns is none of my business, and as for the money, that's their problem where they got it from."

Jesus. He doesn't care. "It *should* be your business, seeing as you stored them in your *house*. That's a dick move if ever I saw one. What if you'd been raided? You'd have gone down for a stretch for handling firearms without a license, especially when the guns are linked to deaths like that. You really didn't think things through, did you? Kaden will likely break under pressure soon. No matter how hard he thinks he is, the kid in him will take over. He'll be scared. Tell the police your name eventually, but it won't do any good, because you won't be at home when the pigs come knocking. You'll be in pieces—in the Thames."

Capo's hands shook down by his sides, his arms, from elbow to shoulder, pinned in place by the ropes. Finally, some kind of reaction. A dark piss stain crept into his grey cargo trousers, the fluid seeping lower and lower as it made its way down his legs.

"Filthy feckin' bastard," Ichabod muttered. "Someone's got tae clean that up. How inconsiderate *are* ye?"

"People like him don't care about that," George said. "They piss wherever they like, marking their territory, except this is the wrong place to do it, because it's *my* territory, mine and my brother's, and you're one dog who doesn't belong in our pack. I think I've had enough of talking to you. I can't stand to even look at you." While George would like to batter ten bells of shit out of the bloke, he needed the anger to deal with Lemon. He nodded at Ichabod.

The Irishman moved so he was side-on to Capo and swung the hammer back. He arced it through the air, the clawed end finding a home in the gang boss' cheekbone, Capo leaning sideways into a dead septuplet from the force. The screams—and not just from Capo, Dipsy was giving his lungs a good old airing an' all—echoed in the big space, and Lemon, at last, looked like things were finally sinking in.

"You'd think," George said over the annoying din, "that me shooting your mates in the head would have been a good indication that I'm not pissing around, Lemon, but maybe a hammer to the face registers better in your brain. Gird your loins, sunshine, because I'm saving you until last, so you're going to have to watch the shit these two will be put through—and know yours will be so much worse."

Lemon closed his eyes.

If he thinks he can shut them when we're dishing out pain, he's got a shock coming.

Ichabod wrenched the hammer out, and Capo screamed some more.

"Let that be a lesson tae ye," Ichabod shouted. "There's more where that came from if ye don't give George what he's really after."

Capo stared at him, his eyebrows scrunched, either from the agony of his cheekbone being smashed and having a hole in it, or because he was that dim, he just didn't get it.

"W-w-what?" he croaked, eyes drooping.

Bollocks. He might pass out. It was just getting fun an' all.

"Think about it." Ichabod wiped the hammer on his forensic suit. A smear of blood in an X joined the spatter from when George had shot the septuplets. "What do ye say tae someone ye've pissed off?"

"S-sorry?"

"That's it. Now say it like ye mean it, else this hammer's goin' in yer other cheek, and then ye'll likely go unconscious, and if George has tae wait even longer for his apology while ye have a kip, I'm goin' tae get *really* narked."

"You're not narked *already*?" Dipsy blurted, his breathing distorted by his clenched teeth. "Oh my God, Capo, you said everything was squared away, that we were okay to deal. Why not just admit it? Come on, we're getting in the shit for your mistake here."

Capo didn't answer.

Ichabod kicked him in the shin. "Give George a proper apology, then!"

"I'm s-sorry. I didn't mean...to go over your heads. I s-should have...should have asked for permission. Please, I'll never do anything like that again."

George smiled. "I know you won't, son." To hit Capo where he suspected it would *really* hurt, he said, "All that money we took from your house. It's going to Jason's family. Thousands and thousands of pounds, and when we've sold your drugs on, they'll get the money from that an' all."

Sick of the sight of him, George shot him in the forehead.

Dipsy cried out like an arachnophobe who'd encountered a spider in his bed, all shrill screams and panic. He brought his legs up then slapped his feet on the floor, rocking back and forth so the chair legs rose.

"You," George said. "Shut your fucking mouth and listen."

Dipsy clamped his lips together, reduced to muted whimpers.

"We've all heard from your dead pals that Capo didn't want you dealing drugs on Judas. How come they knew and you didn't? Why didn't any of them warn you? I'll tell you why: because they didn't fucking like you."

"That's not true. We're all mates."

"Bollocks are you. They didn't care that you'd been rumbled. What was it they said? That even though Capo was the boss, you cut a deal with Prince anyway, as if *you* ran the show. Some boss you had. If it were me, and one of my men called the shots like that, I'd have sliced their throats, yet Capo didn't have the guts to do it. You started selling on Judas when it was still called Golden Eye, didn't you?"

"Yeah."

"I wonder why your boss didn't say so. Why he didn't drop you in it with me, saying it was all your doing like the others did. What's your connection? Why was he loyal to you?"

"I'm not telling you. That's between him and me."

George paced, itching to stab the cricket stump into the shithead's eye. "He sent Lemon to see Goldie to put a stop to you doing things you shouldn't. Was that a shock when you heard the others say that? Capo wanted Goldie to do the dirty work and kill you—so much for your connection. How does it feel to not be wanted in a gang? And, more to the point, why would you *want* to be in a gang where the so-called boss sends his *minion*"—he glanced at Lemon to check his response to the use of that word—"to a leader because he's probably too scared to do it himself? Had no balls to *kill* you himself?"

Lemon didn't even flinch, as expected of someone trained by The Network. George would get the truth out of him about being a minion in the end. It was obvious Lemon was their assassin, but he wanted to know for sure so Janine could keep her eye out in future in case another one took his place and came after her.

"This is all stupid," Dipsy said. "I don't know why he wanted me killed for selling drugs—drugs he *told* me to fucking sell."

"Why did you pick The Golden Eye Estate, eh?"

"Because Goldie's a prick who wouldn't have noticed. Everyone knew he'd taken his eye off the ball before he went missing. I was worried if I kept dealing on Cardigan, you'd get wind."

"You're lying. According to your mates, you all thought you had permission from us. And 'missing', such a good word, don't you think? It gives people the impression Goldie's alive, that he could come back any second, but no, he's not coming back. Prince isn't just running his estate while Goldie has a sabbatical. It being renamed should have been a big indication. He's *dead*. Most people who come to this warehouse are. Only a very few get to walk out of here alive."

Dipsy sniffled. "Oh Jesus, I've got a kid an' that. I've got a *missus*."

"Where was she when our men picked you up from your house?"

"She's staying at her mum's."

"Why?"

"We had a barney."

"Why?"

"*God*, because of me being with the Sparrows, that's why. I had to tell her, she thought I had another woman because I'm not at home until the early hours. I didn't want her leaving me, getting the wrong idea."

George stared at Lemon. "I know another woman who thought her bloke was playing away, too, only he left her with a high rent to pay, which means she doesn't have much money to feed herself and his *baby*."

Lemon didn't seem to care that Becky had obviously been talking. If he did, he hid it well.

George looked at Dipsy. "At least *you've* got some morals. So what's going on with your bird now, then?"

"She's not coming back until I leave the Sparrows, and if I don't, she's telling on me."

"Telling who?"

"You!"

"That's the right answer, because if she wasn't going to tell, we might have had to pay her a little visit to remind her of who her loyalties should be with."

"Please, I'll tell you whatever you want, just leave her alone. She's a good woman."

Another glance at Lemon revealed the man had closed his eyes, likely sensing the end was near for Dipsy.

"I don't think so, Lemon." George strode over to the tool table, threw the cricket stump down, and picked up a heavy-duty stapler. He marched to stand in front of Lemon who now had his eyes wide open. "I told you you're going to watch me inflict pain. It's not your choice whether you witness it or not. When I say how something's going to go, it fucking goes that way, got it?"

Lemon glared at him.

"You've got a serious chip on your shoulder." He glanced at Ichabod. "Get round the back and hold his head steady."

Ichabod dropped the hammer and did as he was told, apparently with relish. He held Lemon's head and bent low to whisper, "I hope, when ye're screamin' in pain, ye wish for death. I want yet tae hope it's all over quickly, knowing it won't be. Ye've got a few things ye need tae give answers on, so it's going tae be a long hour or so. Buckle in for the ride, ye feckin' dickhead, because ye're about tae go on the worst journey of yer life."

George lifted one of Lemon's top eyelids and pressed it to the base of his brow bone, the underside red and wet. He stapled it open, and damn that fucking bastard, he didn't make a sound. George moved on to the next one, repeating the action, and at last, the bloke huffed out a grunt.

George slung the stapler on the floor and addressed Dipsy. "All I need to know is this: are the Sparrows into anything else other than drugs and guns?"

"No. That's it, I swear."

"Did any of you lot know Lemon was employed by The Network?"

"*What*? That shit on the news, the refugee thing?" Dipsy turned his head to gawp at Lemon. "You're a *pervert*? You hurt those poor cows?"

Lemon stared straight ahead.

George patted Dipsy on the top of his head. "You've just earnt yourself a quick death, mate. Tarra." He whipped his gun out and shot him. Then he smiled at Lemon. "Your turn, sunshine."

Chapter Nineteen

Lemon hung from the rack. Naked. His clothes, in a haphazard pile on the floor, seemed to mock him, braying about this final humiliation. It was one thing to anticipate torture, another to endure it with his private parts on show. This shouldn't bother him, but it bloody did. As Minion-66, he'd prided himself as being an easily forgettable man, his face one that people wouldn't glance twice at, mainly due to how he'd walked around as unobtrusively as possible while tailing potential Network employees to see if they were a good fit for the organisation. When out killing, he had the skills and foresight to blend into the crowd afterwards on his way to the flat where he'd holed up until the heat had gone cold. He'd had his dignity intact, no one staring at his knackers, but here, now, he'd been reduced to his base self, maybe even as far back as his teenage years when everything had been embarrassing and he hadn't quite known who he was.

The Irishman stared him up and down, the hammer back in hand. Ichabod, was it? Some weird shit name like that. He smirked at the point his gaze stopped on Lemon's dick—a move designed to bring on a blush so he felt inadequate. Lemon knew that for a fact. He'd looked at Becky that way a hundred times.

Lemon steered his mind away from the humiliation and to his Network phone on the table over there. The prick in front of him had placed it down shortly after they'd all arrived here. Lemon was somehow glad this was the end for him, because once the twins accessed the contact list, had he still been out there living his life, he'd have been on borrowed time anyway. De Luca would be furious as Lemon had direct lines to him on several numbers.

They were going to tell Janine, and she'd find the boss. If not her, then the refugee team assigned to the case. The only person de Luca had left to help him in the force wasn't high up in the team, they weren't anyone who'd be suspected of derailing the investigation, hence de Luca choosing them. They were a 'floater' kind of copper, going where they were needed for short periods, and had recently been sent from their latest prestigious post in another London division to help the refugee officers. Their mind was sharp, and they saw things in ways the others didn't. They stayed under the radar in this current position, had been told to avoid being seen by Janine, because that bitch would wonder why that particular person had been moved from their other job. She'd ask questions. And ultimately, she'd work out what was going on.

With no clue as to the time, Lemon couldn't judge whether de Luca would send an angry diatribe soon, demanding to know why he hadn't checked in yet about Janine and Dipsy. George would home in on the message alert and inspect the burner. He'd see the numbers, maybe even ring one of them. At least that way de Luca would know something was up and get the fuck out of London if George spoke.

Lemon wanted The Network to continue, to thrive. He was of the same mind as de Luca—women needed to know their place, and the thought of them basically being kidnapped and taken to other countries had given him many a hard-on. He'd even sampled a few of them, the newbies, ones who had to be taught with punches and kicks that they weren't doing it right. He'd enjoyed his time teaching them how to please a man. Enjoyed even more how they'd cried and clawed at him in their attempts to push him off. Their fight was part of the excitement, which was why Becky had never done it for him in the sack, and neither had his previous ex. He wanted more. Violence, domination, the ultimate power, so much so that any woman other than a refugee with hatred in her heart paled by comparison.

He owed de Luca a lot, the man allowing him to indulge in what some would call depraved fantasies. De Luca knew what a *real* man wanted, and he made a lot of money out of it. It would be a sin if he were caught.

Would it have hit the airwaves already that the new refugee house had been found? The police would be stupid to release such information, alerting The Network that they had to maintain their mundane lives for a while longer. Alerting de Luca, so he could fly off into the sunset again and live wherever he now lived.

Would the mole in the refugee team have been called in to help interview the women? Or would they be asleep still, going into work in a few hours to find their part in this had been revealed, the new refugee house man spilling the copper's name? If the twins caught up with de Luca, after scouring his phone with everyone's burner numbers in it, it wouldn't be long before the mole, and everyone else, was outed.

Lemon shouldn't care, he was facing death, after all, but to have been with such an intricate organisation for so long, to be revered, held in awe…losing it would be a bitter pill that would choke him.

The manacles dug into his wrists and ankles, rubbing, and bowing his back to stop the spikes digging in so much took a lot of energy. He had to hold himself taut, and any lack of concentration had his body slumping, the spikes giving him a sharp poke, reminding him where he was and that the Irishman still stared at his meat and two veg. What the fuck was up with him? Was he a secret pervert, too? Lemon clenched his arse cheeks then regretted it. The bullet had lodged there, and pain barked into his muscles.

He shifted his attention to the Sparrows. Only Vanga wasn't here to take his punishment, which pissed Lemon off. None of the others had grassed him up while being spoken to—saying that, they didn't know where he was and what he'd been sent to do. But he'd return home eventually, and the twins' men would haul him in. Maybe he'd have Becky's death to pay for on top of everything else. Would Vanga kill Noah, though, or just leave him crying wherever Becky was staying? Becky's parents would then have to take the kid in, bring him up, likely cursing because they enjoyed their freedom now their daughter was an adult. Mum wouldn't offer to have him, she was convinced Noah wasn't even his. His mother had no problem turning a blind eye when it suited her, and she'd tell the Suttons to fuck off if they expected her help.

She'd be devastated to find out he'd gone missing, which was the line he reckoned George would take. Now Lemon suspected Janine was bent for the twins, he thought the two mad bastards had killed Sykes, letting his wife think The Network had done it. Would that happen to Lemon? Would his body be deposited somewhere with a note, the same as what had happened with the Polish bird Goldie had kept locked up in his loft? Lemon had de Luca's ear, the boss regularly telling him things about the Users. He'd said it was so Lemon was up to date with the goings-on so he was ready to go with information if he was needed to kill. There was so much stored in his head that he could pass on to The Brothers. Did he want to? No. De Luca had given him the chance to be his true self for a few years, and he wouldn't do anything to jeopardise The Network. Not anything within his control anyway.

That phone, though… It would bring the whole lot tumbling down.

George, who'd been browsing a line of tools on the table, looked over and smiled. "I'm trying to decide what would hurt the most."

Lemon stared at the tools. A mace, the handle wooden, the spikes silver. Some other things he'd never seen before and couldn't even imagine their uses.

George picked one of them up. "I was having a browse last week and came across this site about medieval torture devices. The Dark Ages, a bloody time, where they seemed to enjoy inflicting pain. Like me. I got bored with the usual tools so found this site that recreates the sort of thing I need. This is my favourite. It's called the Pear of Anguish, otherwise known as the choke or mouth pear."

He picked up a device that had metal strips making up the pear shape, much like the long, narrow wings of a dragonfly. George screwed something at the top, and the wings expanded, creating a claw-like end.

"See how that opens up like a flower showing off its petals?" George sounded odd, nothing like he had before, as if he'd gone into some kind of weird state. Fascinated by the weapon. His head cocked the same as an eagle spotting its dinner.

"It was usually used on women, witches, shoved exactly where you might imagine, and the more the screw is turned, the more the petals open. The pain must have been awful when the width got bigger than a baby's head." He smiled and stroked one of the wings. "I bet it'd ming, me opening it up in your arse."

Lemon swallowed. This bloke was insane.

George placed the thing down and selected another, what appeared to be black iron tongs, the bits on the ends in the shape of a U, two-pronged claws, the tips pointed and facing inwards, towards each other, a bit like the jaws of a digger. Tweezers with added menace, and bigger. Lemon shuddered. What the fuck was *that* used for?

George grinned. "This is a breast ripper or the Iron Spider. They warmed it up, which reminds me, I have a heat gun there, so that'll do if I fancy doing it their way. D'you know what they used to do with it? Grip a woman's tits, the claws sinking in, then they'd rip the fuckers off. A nasty load of bastards, those people back then. I reckon it'd work just as well on your bollocks."

He turned, pressing the tongs together so the sharp tips tapped against each other, snapping teeth. "There's this other thing, but it hasn't arrived yet. Still being made. It cost a fortune, but I've got a feeling it'll be worth it. Old Henry the Eighth might have commissioned it, because it was used in his time. Have you heard of the rack? It stretched people. This does the opposite. The Scavenger's Daughter, invented by some bloke called Leonard Skeffington, who I'd like to have met because he seems my sort of fella. Are you enjoying the history lesson? Nah, you're not, are you. Fucking tough."

Lemon didn't want to hear about people from years ago. He wanted this over.

"This thing I'm on about," George went on, "is an upright circle of steel, and you have to kneel in it, then lower your belly to your thighs. Someone, me for example, would twist the big screw in the top, which slowly makes the circle smaller. It squeezes you, constricts all your body parts, the organs, and in the end, your lungs can barely fill. If you don't confess, you end up dying from lack of air. Shame it didn't arrive in time for you."

He walked over, standing beside Ichabod, and it made sense now, why the Irishman had been staring at Lemon's cock. He'd known which tool George was going to use first, and he'd likely been imagining how the Iron Spider would claw his privates off. A kick to the nuts was bad enough, and Lemon didn't want to think about how much it would hurt having them ripped off.

No matter what, he wasn't going to provide the one thing they wanted. He might scream in pain, but he'd never give them de Luca's name.

They could fucking well find it on their own.

Chapter Twenty

George was well pleased with his new gadgets. There were a few he hadn't explained to Lemon, but others would get the pleasure of his little schoolroom teachings into the history of people who'd enjoyed inflicting pain. He'd use the Iron Spider and the Pear of Anguish on the Minion, see if they got him talking.

He moved close to Lemon and relaxed his grip so the claws at the end of the tongs sprang open. He positioned them either side of Lemon's crown jewels, smiling at the man's increased breathing speed, his dick wobbling where he was shaking so much.

"You've got a small package there, or is that because you're shitting yourself and it's shrivelled in fear?" He stared up into Lemon's eyes. "Now, before I do anything, I'll ask a question. Who the *fuck* do you think you are, treating Becky the way you did?"

Lemon sneered down at him. "She had to learn her place."

"Excuse me?"

"She had too much of a mind of her own. Women need taming."

"Did you ever care about her?"

Lemon's eyes took on a hard glint. "No. I used her as a cover. People wouldn't suspect me if I had a woman. The kid, he was an unwelcome little bastard, and I hope the pair of them fucking die when—"

Alarm bells sounded. "When what?"

Lemon clamped his lips.

George relaxed, remembering where Becky was. "She's having a little holiday, safe from you, so if you think you're going to rile me, you can fuck off."

Lemon smirked. Mind games, that's what he was playing.

George squeezed the tongs so the claw tips rested either side of Lemon's tackle. "It's clear you've got no respect for women. Fuck some refugees, did you?"

"More than my fair share."

"So you *are* in with The Network."

Lemon let out a harsh laugh. "I won't insult your intelligence by saying no."

"So you're the one who went round bumping everyone off, including Beaker, a young bloke who worked for us."

"And?"

Oh, this bloke was a ballsy bastard. He had a torture device kissing his twig and berries, yet his arrogance remained. Had his mother brought him up to purposely instil her own sense of self-importance into him? Becky had said this Faith woman was a cow, which reminded him, they had to pay her a visit.

"Who's your boss?" George asked.

"I'll never tell you, so you may as well get on with doing whatever it is you have planned."

"Maybe this will change your mind."

George squeezed the tongs, the claws sinking into the soft flesh of Lemon's bollocks, and he kept squeezing until the tips met inside them. Lemon snorted through the pain, maybe taking his mind to another place so the agony didn't register, and fuck, George admired his restraint.

And hated himself for it.

He took a step back, then another, then wrenched, hard. The skin ripped, the balls coming away from his body, and George held his prize up, blood dripping down the tong handles to coat his glove. Lemon still did nothing but snort, saliva dribbling from the corners of his mouth, the wound pissing blood, his cock a lonely little bastard without its two companions.

"He's got some way of ignorin' the pain, masterin' it," Ichabod muttered. "Maybe he was taught it by his boss. Either way, impressive."

George nodded and opened the Iron Spider, letting the flesh and two testes fall out of their sacs to the floor. He stood on them, twisting his foot, and laughed at Lemon releasing a groan, as if they were still attached to him and he could feel what George was doing.

"You're a strong boy," George said. "What are you doing, trying to prove I can't break you? You've already told me most of what I needed to know without me even trying. I'd have thought you'd be silent, but oh, I forgot you've got an ego the size of England, so of course you'd want to get your point across. You may have been The Network's assassin in London, but as for the other aspects of your life, you're nothing but scum."

He walked over to the table, placed the Spider down, and picked up the Pear. Chuckling to himself, he dragged the stepladder away from the wall and opened it in front of Lemon, climbing a couple of steps so he could reach his mouth easily.

"Open your gob."

"Fuck you."

"Oh dear. We've got ourselves a stubborn little twat, Ich. Go and get the mace and the shears, will you?"

Lemon's eyes watered, the upper, exposed lids dry where he couldn't blink.

Ichabod, tools at the ready, stood beside the stepladder. "Just let me know when."

"Now will do."

Lemon looked down, as did George. Ichabod put the mace by his feet and opened the shears, putting the blades above and below the shrivelled sausage that had given up trying to look like a dick. Lemon's breathing turned into short, sharp pants, and he raised his head, clearly not wanting to give them the satisfaction of him seeing what was going to happen. George grabbed Lemon's hair and pulled his head down so he had no choice but to see it. Ichabod squeezed the handles, and the blades sliced through, the cock falling off and landing on the floor. Lemon whimpered, his teeth gritted, tears streaming down his cheeks. He breathed through his nose, snot making it difficult, nostrils flaring, and clenched his fists.

"*Something's* got to hurt," George said.

Ichabod dropped the shears, swiped up the mace, and stabbed the spikes into Lemon's groin wound. He scraped them over the open flesh repeatedly, creating little ravines, blood filling them then oozing downwards.

"It looks like you're brushing someone's fucking *hair*," George said, laughing.

Lemon didn't find that funny. He glared at George, his lips pursed, cheeks soaked from his eyes leaking. "If I wasn't on this fucking rack, I swear, I'd go for you."

"But you *are* on the rack. Am I meant to be scared?" George taunted. "Because even if you weren't up there, I wouldn't rate your chances with me."

Ichabod used the mace like a cricket bat and swung it into the bleeding mass. Lemon's mouth opened, and before it shut, George shoved the closed-petal Pear inside it. He twisted the screw on the end, the lips stretching, the device expanding. Another screw turn or two, and the lips split at the corners, blood trailing down Lemon's chin. George screwed some more, sensed the moment the teeth broke, *heard* the delicious crack as the molars either side pushed outwards from the pressure.

Lemon finally screeched.

"That's better, my old son," George said. "They say toothache is one of the worst pains and can bring a man to his knees. You making that racket, that's all I needed to hear."

He removed the Pear, climbed down, and took the mace off Ichabod and picked up the shears. Lemon cried quietly, blood streaming from his mouth. Satisfied he'd broken the bastard, George took the tools back to the table. He could saw him up while he was alive, but he'd done it so many times before that he fancied a bit of a change. He chose an extra-long cheese wire and got back on the stepladder, staring Lemon in his eyelid-stapled eyes.

"There, there, it'll all be over soon. Just know I'm doing this for Becky and Noah. She dobbed you in to us, by the way, in case you hadn't worked it out already, so she *wasn't* afraid of you at all. You *didn't* break her or show the woman her place."

He threaded one cutter handle behind Lemon, anticipating the bloke spitting at him, but with his mouth wrecked, his lower region a mess, and his arse likely still throbbing from that bullet, he obviously didn't have the energy. With both wooden handles of the cutter gripped in his fingers, he crossed the wire, swapped hands, and wrenched. The thin steel sank into Lemon's neck, through the Adam's apple, and George applied more pressure, watching the light leaving the bastard's eyes.

"I always get them in the end, sunshine." George grinned. "Always."

George went to work slicing the bodies up. Ichabod and Greg got on with putting the bits into black bags and tipping them into the Thames. All but Lemon, who'd be left somewhere later.

Between revs of the saw, a phone chirruped, and they all glanced over at the tool table. The burner phone Ichabod had found in Lemon's SUV turned in a circle from the vibration. George put the saw down, stripped his gloves off, and went over to see who'd sent a message.

It didn't have a name attached to it, but it didn't need one. What it did need was a fucking dictionary, because the message was in some kind of code. Praying the translation was on the phone somewhere, he prodded open a few apps, then came across one called NETWORK WORDS. He pressed the icon, and a dictionary opened. He didn't have time to fuck about trying to match the shorthand and symbols into words.

"Fuck it!"

"What's the matter?" Ichabod asked.

"The message is fucking bollocks. I can't read it."

Greg came over, stared at the screen, and sighed. "Are you thick, bruv?"

George didn't bother acknowledging that. "What aren't I seeing?"

"The button with the word 'translate' on it." Greg sniffed. "It might well turn the messages into English."

George pressed it then went back to the message. "Well, fuck me. If he didn't need it on translate, then he knows the code off by heart."

UNKNOWN: HAVE ALL THE GOODS BEEN DISPATCHED?

Would George need to write his response in code? If he used English, would the sender know it might not be Lemon? He typed out his answer.

GEORGE: NO.

Holding his breath, he waited for a reply.

UNKNOWN: ARE YOU PICKING HER UP TOMORROW INSTEAD?

"Thank fuck for that," George muttered, relieved the message had gone through without suspicion.

"For what?" Greg asked.

"It doesn't matter."

GEORGE: NEEDED TO ENSURE IT WAS SAFE AT ALL LOCATIONS SO HAVEN'T ENTERED HER PROPERTY YET.

UNKNOWN: ARE YOU AT LEAST ON YOUR WAY TO THE BITCH?

GEORGE: YES. IF THERE'S NO RISK WHEN I GET THERE, I'LL DO IT. IF IT SEEMS UNSAFE, WILL ABORT UNTIL TOMORROW.

UNKNOWN: MESSAGE THE OTHERS. I HAVEN'T HEARD FROM THEM EITHER.

GEORGE: IT'S A BIG JOB. THEY'RE PROBABLY TOO BUSY. THE WOMEN MIGHT BE PLAYING UP. WILL MAKE CONTACT. STILL IN THE BIG SMOKE?

UNKNOWN: AFFIRMATIVE.

GEORGE: NEED A MEET.

UNKNOWN: WHAT FOR?

GEORGE: TO DISCUSS A WOMAN.

UNKNOWN: COME TO THE WALKER HOTEL IN SHOREDITCH AT ELEVEN A.M. WOMAN WILL BE WAITING.

"Got you," George said.

Greg smiled. "Janine will be pleased."

Ichabod rubbed his forehead with the back of his gloved hand. "Especially if ye get hold of his phone."

"With all The Network employees' numbers on it." George put the burner down. "Even if we only get the ones in London, we'll have cut off the head of the snake."

"It could be the complete fall of The Network without him," Ichabod said.

George nodded. "Thank fuck."

At four a.m., George posed Lemon's body against a lamppost outside the DCI's house. He'd asked Ichabod to write a note to put in Lemon's pocket; they hadn't bothered dressing him, but George had placed the folded items beside the twat, knowing full well the pockets would be checked. He would have left the burner phone there, too, but he needed it in case The Network boss made contact again to change the time and location of the meet. He dropped the penis in Lemon's lap and walked back to the stolen van.

Driving around for a while, he parked in a side street and used a burner to phone the police. Scottish once again, he gave the man the details and ended the call, throwing the SIM out of the window.

At the breaker's yard, he dropped the van off to their man who'd come in early to crush it, then he burnt his forensic clothing in a nearby oil drum. Hungry after the night's work, he used the yard loo, washing his face, swilling the sink round afterwards to get rid of the diluted blood. He sat in the portacabin and ate a Pot Noodle, listening to the sound of the crusher doing its work.

Next door in the other cabin, he left an envelope on the desk as payment. Then he walked home, whistling quietly, wanting to get some notes down before they met with the Network tosser.

He'll have a fucking shock when he sees me.

Chapter Twenty-One

Becky had met other men, and women, like Mr Tomlinson several times in her life since the stabbing but thankfully had been able to steer herself away from their orbit. An adult now, she'd decided to join the racism group and lend her support. Everyone was so kind. White people also attended, and it was clear they disagreed with how some people

behaved. It gave Becky hope that things could change, that one day they could all live in peace.

She wasn't stupid, though. It would never happen. Racism would be passed down from generation to generation for years to come.

The meeting over, she declined to go for a meal afterwards with Mum and Dad and the Gupta family. Daksh had moved away a long time ago, and without him there to talk to she'd be a bit bored. Instead, she decided to go to the pub along the way, have a quick glass of wine, then go home to bed.

The Hog's Nose had a lively crowd, the music throbbing, and Becky had to elbow her way to the bar. She stood between an old man perched on a stool and a drunk woman whose lipstick had smeared. Too many kisses? Becky smiled, luckily catching the barman's eye, and got served quickly. She turned and glanced around, looking for a place to sit, but all the tables were full. It reminded her how alone she was without Daksh, how she didn't trust anyone else to be her friend. Drinking by herself had become normal.

"Standing room only," someone said in her ear.

She moved round so she could see who'd spoken, vaguely recognising the man. Did he live round here? She racked her brains to work out if she'd been to school with him, but he must have gone to the other secondary, because she couldn't place him.

"Lemon," he said.

"Pardon?" She blinked at his random word.

"That's my name. Lemon."

"Your surname?"

"Obviously." He grinned. "Fancy coming outside with me? We can chat while I have a fag."

He seemed nice enough, and others would be outside, too, so it wasn't like she'd be in any danger. She nodded at him and followed him out the back to the beer garden. A few other people sat around, drinking and puffing, smoke rising. In the warm night, she sat at one of the wooden tables and sipped her wine, Lemon sitting opposite and sparking up. He blew the smoke away from her face, which told her he had manners.

"I like a bit of black," he said.

She reared her head back, unsure if she should feel pleased about what he'd said or offended. On one hand, his statement told her he didn't dislike black people, but on the other…rude much?

"Um, not the sort of line I'd advise you using," she said.

He slapped a hand to his forehead. "Shit, sorry, I was just letting you know I fancy you."

"Then you should have just said that. No need to mention my skin."

"Bollocks, I always put my foot in it. Sorry again. Seriously." He made an eek face, rubbing a hand up and down his thigh. Embarrassed?

She smiled; he seemed genuinely contrite. Maybe she could overlook what he'd said. "Just be mindful of what you say in future, that's all."

She'd never stop sticking up for her rights. Like she'd told Mr Tomlinson, she wouldn't shut up if people were racist, and if Lemon was being sly, hiding his true beliefs, putting her down with his comment, basically fetishising her skin colour, she wouldn't put up with it. That shit was up there with people always thinking they could touch her hair without permission. Also, Mr Tomlinson had touched Daksh even though he'd hated his skin colour, so who was to say this Lemon bloke wasn't the same?

She'd have to be careful. On her guard.

"I will," he said. "Maybe you can educate me on how to behave around you."

Another waving red flag. "Err, no, you need to educate yourself. It's not my job to teach you anything."

"Fair enough." He sucked on his cigarette. "So, what's a pretty girl like you doing in a place like this on your own?"

"Having a drink."

He laughed, the sound unsteady, as if he wasn't sure how to take her. "I gathered that. Christ, you don't half make things difficult, don't you."

She frowned. "What do you mean?"

"Well, you didn't go all gooey and giggle when I said that."

"You asked me a question, and I answered it."

"Am I wasting my time here or what?"

"It depends how much work you're prepared to put into getting me to stick around once I've finished my wine."

"Ah, you're the strong, independent type. I get it." He paused and stared at her. "You're bloody gorgeous, you know that?"

She had to admit, the way he looked at her, well, that hadn't happened before. Nor had anyone other than her parents or Auntie Sheila told her she was gorgeous. She'd have to watch him. He was dangerous. She might end up liking him.

Was that such a bad thing?

"Do you use that chat-up line on every girl you meet?" she asked.

He threw his hands up in mock despair. "Come on, love, give me a break here. I'm trying!"

She laughed. "What do you do for a living?"

He shrugged. "A bit of this, a bit of that."

"Doesn't sound too promising."

"After a man with money, are you, because I've got plenty of that."

"Money makes no odds to me."

"That's what they all say."

She finished her wine in two gulps and stood. "Look, I don't know why you bothered asking me to come out here. You've got a bit of an attitude about you."

"Please, sit back down. I'm a dick. Sorry. I'm not good at this chatting-up lark." He stubbed his cigarette out on the ground, grinding it with his Timberland heel. "Let me buy you another drink. Start again."

Faith was what would be considered an acquired taste. What she really was? Racist. Becky had sensed it the moment she'd followed Lemon into his mother's kitchen for the first time and Faith had clocked her. The shock on her face had spoken volumes.

They'd spent an awkward ten minutes drinking a cup of tea, Faith acting as if Becky wasn't there, directing all of her questions to her son—who didn't pull his mum up on the fact she was being rude. This didn't bode well, and Becky had the urge to get up and walk out—more red flags, ones she shouldn't ignore. If, after a month of them seeing each other, Lemon wasn't prepared to stand up for her, would he ever do that?

His relationship with Faith seemed to be her dominating and him acquiescing. He was a strong-willed bloke, so how come he turned into a wet lettuce in Faith's presence? Becky understood that you always felt like a child with your parents, no matter whether they treated you like an adult, but this was a bizarre situation.

"So what have you been up to lately?" Faith asked Lemon.

Becky wasn't giving him the chance to answer. "We've been going out a lot, getting to know each other."

Faith gave her a mean glare. "I wasn't asking you."

"I know." Becky smiled. "You've been rude since I arrived, ignoring me, so I thought I'd remind you I'm actually here."

Faith swung her gaze to Lemon. "Are you going to let her speak to me like that, son?"

Lemon laughed. "She's got a point, though…"

"Well I never." Faith huffed. "In all my years on this earth, I never expected to be disrespected by a n—"

Silence filled the pause.

"By a what?" Becky asked, because it didn't seem like Lemon was going to come to her defence. She'd have to stand up for herself.

"New girlfriend," Faith said. "The last one wasn't like you."

"Oh, she wasn't black?" Becky sighed.

"No."

"I see." Becky nudged Lemon. Raised her eyebrows.

"Look, Mum," Lemon said, "I like Becky. Doesn't matter what you think."

Faith's cheeks flared red. "It should. I'm your mother, and considering what your father did…"

"Doesn't give you the right to dictate who I see, though, does it," he said and got up to open the fridge and take out a Victoria sponge. "You said you'd made this for us?"

"Put it back," Faith muttered.

"Why?" Lemon frowned.

"Because I don't want you to have it now."

Becky knew what she was really saying. "She means she doesn't want me to have any, Lemon. My black arse doesn't deserve a white woman's cake." She levelled her gaze at Faith. "It's okay, you can say it. I've heard it all before. I'd rather you were real about your feelings than hide your racist heart. We'll all know where we stand then, won't we."

Faith sniffed. "You're probably a good person, but…"

Becky laughed. "Wow. Okay. It wasn't nice to meet you. I'll be off now."

She walked out, expecting Lemon to follow her, but at the end of his street, when she peered over her shoulder, he wasn't there. What should she do about that? Have a go at him? Tell him she was the main woman in his life now and his mum had to take a back seat? But what if he'd stayed behind to have a go at Faith? What if he was defending Becky right now?

She waited on the corner for half an hour, and with no sign of Lemon, she went home. A man who didn't defend her wasn't any man at all. And she'd be telling him that next time she saw him.

"All right, I'll admit it, she's a weird one," Lemon said later that night in the pub. "And besides, I wanted a bit of that cake. She makes a banging sponge."

Becky stared at him. "Are you for real?"

"What?" he said on laugh. "What did I do wrong?"

"If you don't know, then there's no hope for you."

He leant back. Sipped some lager. "Oh, was it you being upset that she didn't want you to have a slice?"

Becky blinked several times. Surely he'd heard her say about a black person not being allowed a white person's cake. Had it gone over his head? Hadn't he picked up on the racism at all apart from telling his mother he liked Becky and it was none of Faith's business?

"She's so rude," Becky said.

Lemon shrugged. "It's just her way."

"And that makes it okay, does it?"

"It was just cake, Bec."

"It wasn't about the fucking cake," she hissed.

He frowned. "I don't get what the problem is, then. I basically told her to butt out."

She leant back herself, staring at him in bemusement, confusion, and outright shock. He really didn't get it. Had no idea.

Maybe she should rethink things. Stop seeing him.

"I'll make it all better." He fiddled in his jacket's big pocket and produced a package wrapped in rose-printed paper. Handed it over. Smiled.

"Presents don't fix things that go so deep," she said.

"Listen, we won't go round Mum's again, not together anyway. She's an odd one, I'll give you that, and whatever happened back there, let's forget it and move on."

Forget that he'd left her standing on the corner? That he didn't even pick up on the real undertones in the conversation—or Becky revealing why his mother didn't want them to have that bastard cake? Did he think that by telling Faith he liked Becky, that was enough?

She peeled back the paper. He'd bought her a book. But not just any book. It was an old copy of Beauty and the Beast, one she knew must have cost a fortune. She'd mentioned her love of the story to him one night a couple of weeks ago, how it resonated with her because Belle had fallen in love with who the person was inside, not what he looked like. She hadn't thought he'd been listening, not properly anyway, but clearly, he had.

"Oh," she said quietly. "Oh…"

"D'you like it?" he asked.

"I love it."

He couldn't be that bad, could he? Not if he'd bought her this. He'd chosen what was important to her instead of buying earrings or a necklace.

Maybe there was hope for him yet and all those red flags might turn green.

Once Lemon had left her and Noah, Becky had gone over their time together. Spotted how he'd dimmed her light. Dragged her down. The signs had been there from the start, her instinct spot-on, yet his behaviour after he'd treated her offhandedly had blinded her into thinking he could change, be the person she wished he could be—who she hoped everyone was inside. He'd be cruel then charming, easy to get along with. In the weeks before he'd buggered off, he'd taken to blowing cigarette smoke in her face instead of directing it away from her, laughing if her eyes watered. He'd taken her round to Faith's, despite saying they didn't have to go.

And he'd stolen the book and sold it, drinking the proceeds in the pub with Vanga, coming home rat-arsed and calling her names. Lazy. Stupid. A bitch.

Why had she allowed herself to be taken in by him?

Because she'd wanted her own fairy tale.

Sadly, it had all been nothing but lies.

Chapter Twenty-Two

Her captor still hadn't gone, and it was five a.m., the sunrise lightening the curtains. He hadn't said much for the past couple of hours, maybe pondering his options in between sending texts, but he'd left it too late if he wanted to leave in the darkness. Did he plan to keep her here until he could get away tonight? What the hell would they *do* all day? Just sit around? She'd need to have the cuffs off to deal with Noah. Would he allow that?

"If you go now," she said, "not many people will be on the roads."

"I've been waiting for a reply from Lemon. The stupid prick's probably asleep."

"He told you to leave before the sun comes up. Shouldn't you do as he asked if you're worried about him killing people? He might kill you if you don't do what he said."

"He said I could kill *you* if I wanted."

Her heart leapt in fear. "Do you? Want to?"

"Fuck, no."

"Then you're a better person than him."

She studied him now a little light had come in, but it was still too murky to make anything out other than the skin through the holes in the balaclava. He was white, she'd worked that much out, but so much of him was still a mystery to her. If he was staying, and if Noah woke up at his usual time of about eight, she'd be able to see him better. The curtains weren't lined, and if the day turned out as sunny as yesterday afternoon, it'd be light enough.

"Can I use the toilet?" she asked. She'd been holding it for a while now, and her bladder hurt.

"Yeah. I could do with a piss myself, but I can't exactly leave you out here, can I."

He followed her into the bathroom.

"Um, can you wait outside? You could leave the door open." She needed it open in case he took it upon himself to go and see Noah. She didn't want him anywhere near her son. If she could see where he was going, she'd try to stop him.

"Fine."

He stood side-on, and she cursed him for not turning his back. If he'd faced the other way, she could have hit him, pushed him, grabbing the giraffe and striking him with it. Cheeks hot from embarrassment, she sat and did a wee, finishing up by washing her hands. A thin hand towel hung on a silver hoop. Was it long enough to do what she wanted with it?

She dried her hands, going through the scenario in her mind. He strode towards the chair, and she took her chance. She got as close as she could and, the ends of the concertinaed towel in each hand, flicked the curve of material over his head, and pulled it against his throat. He lifted one hand in an attempt to get it off his neck, losing his balance and landing on his knees. She let go and ran to snatch up the giraffe. She approached again and walloped him, a crack sounding, too loud for it not to have been a dangerous blow.

Shit. What if she'd killed him? She'd only meant to knock him out so she could get Noah and drive away. What if she now had to go through life like Daksh, having killed someone to save herself?

He flopped facedown on the floor, groaning. Relieved he'd made a noise, she stood at his back so if he wanted to grab her, he'd have to turn, giving her time to move away. He continued moaning. Quickly, she managed to slide her hands through the cuffs by folding her thumbs under. She had to see how badly he was injured. Whether or not he was dying. The outcome of her visual examination would determine what she did next. She couldn't phone the police, it would have to be The Brothers.

She put the cuffs on the sideboard, flicked the light on, and stared at him. The balaclava, the thin type, nylon not wool, had a wet patch at the back that had to be blood. She spotted his gun, he must have dropped it at some point, and picked it up, aiming it at him as she walked to the top of his head. She bent and ripped the balaclava off, jumping back in shock. *Vanga* lay on the floor, Lemon's best friend, a man who'd come to their house and stayed for dinner, watched films, or played board games. The bastard had disguised his voice so she wouldn't know it was him.

She hadn't known he was this kind of man, but now she did, and it made sense why *he'd* come to warn her. Lemon must have told him that he'd let Becky know about the Sparrows, what with them being mates and everything, and Vanga had agreed to watch her, scare her.

She dropped the balaclava. "You fucking *arsehole*, Vanga."

Unafraid now she knew it was him, she moved to stand in front of him, a couple of metres back, and pointed the gun at him—only to scare him, she wouldn't shoot unless she thought Noah was in danger. Vanga didn't laugh to indicate she held a fake. His eyes widened, and he shook his head a little, giving her proof she had the real deal in her double grip.

"Don't," he said.

"I can't believe you said you'd rape me and kill my baby." It came out as a whisper.

How sad that someone she'd considered a good man harboured gross ideas in his head—he had to have those tendencies to have said it in the first place, didn't he? It just went to show you could never fully know someone, not really.

"Who knows you're here?" she asked and tightened her finger on the trigger.

"Hold up! That's racked, you stupid cow." He managed to sit up.

She didn't know what that meant. "What?"

"The gun, it's racked, which means the bullets are ready to go, and if you pull the trigger, it'll fire."

She eased how tight she held it. "Maybe that's what I want. Maybe I *want* to shoot your fucking brains out for being such a sneaky bastard. You *know* me, I thought we were friends."

"Yeah, well, you know what thought did, don't you." He stared at the gun. "There's no silencer, so it'll be loud, but if you want people to come running and catch you, be my guest."

"You should be worried about them seeing *you*. You should have gone home when it was dark. Did you think I was just going to sit here all day and take whatever you dished out? That I wasn't going to retaliate? Jesus."

"You shouldn't have hit me again. Lemon's going to go ape."

"I don't give a fuck. This place belongs to one of the twins' mates, so he'll deal with any fallout."

But what he'd said made sense. She didn't need people to come snooping, regardless of whether it could be hushed up, especially now it wasn't night-time anymore.

"It'd be too late anyway," he said. "The police would be called before The Brothers' friend could get here; the people in the other chalets would hear the gun go off. Fuck, my head's banging."

She wouldn't shoot him unless she absolutely had to, but she could hit him until he blacked out, tie him up. She inched behind him again, put the gun on the dining table, and picked up the giraffe. The back of his head *did* have a hole it in, about an inch wide, and fresh blood oozed like thick doughnut jam. A large bump and small wound indicated where she'd hit him the last time. Now she wasn't afraid for her life, acting in self-defence, could she deliberately hurt him again? Could she once again hide another death?

Noah popped into her mind.

Yes, she bloody could.

She struck Vanga hard, twice, and he flopped to the floor, his eyes closed. Was he pretending to be asleep? Cautious, in case he gripped her as she went past, she skirted around him and put the giraffe on the coffee table. She picked up a velvet throw blanket off the sofa and sped past him into the kitchen, finding scissors to cut strips down the width, watching him all the while. He still hadn't moved, so she reckoned he was out of it. His chest rose and fell, though, so she wasn't a murderer.

She gathered all of her courage, keeping Noah in the forefront of her mind, and it gave her the guts to take Vanga's hands and place them together so she could tie his wrists. She waited for him to spring up, to knock her backwards, but he remained out of it. Next, she secured his ankles, leaving him on the floor, his blood seeping onto the white tiles and creeping along the top of one, the grout turning red. She heaved at the smell that puffed up.

Hands washed at the kitchen sink using Fairy liquid, she dried them on a tea towel and went into the bedroom. Noah slept on, thankfully oblivious, and she closed the door, returning to the sofa to make a call.

George answered. "What's up?"

"Vanga broke in and said he was going to rape me."

"Fuck me, are you all right?"

"I am now."

"How the fuck did he know where you were?"

"He followed me. He knows I went to see you at Debbie's, which means *Lemon* knows. He's unconscious on the floor. I hit him with a giraffe and—"

George breathed for a few seconds. "A *giraffe*?"

"It's an ornament. He has a gun. I've touched it."

"Calm down and sit tight. Our mate will be with you shortly. Did he hurt you or Noah?"

"No, just scared me. He's a Sparrow."

"I know. He's the only one we haven't found to put under surveillance. The rest are all dead, so no more worries for you. Faith will have a visit, so even she won't bother you."

"Oh God, oh God, okay. He knows I went to Yiannis' shop earlier to get food for my holiday. He's been watching me. He's got a *hole* in his head."

"Serves him right, and that's nothing compared to what happened to Lemon."

"What did you do?" The words were out before she could stop them. *Did* she want to know the answer?

"Put it this way, he doesn't possess a dick anymore."

"Jesus Christ, you chopped it off?"

"Look, go and make a cuppa. Our mate will let himself in. He's about sixty, got grey hair, but don't let that fool you. He's one of them ninja blokes, good with karate and whatever. He's called Orion, obviously not his real name. Let me get on and phone him. As I said, sit tight, and if he wakes, use that giraffe on him again."

He hung up, and she stared from the phone to Vanga, who still hadn't moved. She checked on Noah again, then made a cuppa, keeping her eye on Vanga. She leant on the kitchen cabinet and drank, her eyes blurring because she stared at him too hard. This shit had dredged up all of her feelings regarding her past. Not only had she been involved when someone else had killed a man, she could very well end up being a killer if Vanga snuffed it.

Just as she finished the last mouthful of tea, a key scraped in the lock, and she let out a pathetic scream.

A suave-looking grey-haired man appeared, glanced at Vanga, and laughed. "What a fucking plonker. Are you all right, gal?"

"I-I did that. He…"

"I know. But I don't want to hear about him, I want to hear about you. *Are you all right*?"

She nodded, although tears brimmed, the enormity of the situation catching up with her.

"You'll get over it, given time."

"I won't."

"Been in this situation before, have you?"

"Sort of."

"Well, then, I'll say the worry fades. Doesn't completely go, but it isn't so in your face."

"True. I need to leave. I can't stay here."

"As it happens, I own a caravan park up the road as well as this place, so I've brought some keys. Take that nipper of yours to Sundown Peaks about a mile away. I assume you've got a satnav or you can use a phone for Google Maps?"

She nodded.

"Right. Your van is two hundred and three— it's one reserved for people who need to lie low. I'll deal with this shitbag. George is aware of where I'm sending you. My son will follow in his car to make sure you're not tailed, and he'll stick with you throughout your stay."

"He'll be in the caravan *with* me?"

"Nah, he'll park beside it and sit in the car. Red SUV, registration number I B 40. Fuck knows why he felt the need to let everyone know his age, but there you go. You can create a child and hope for the best but still end up with a dickhead."

He came over and gave her the keys, resting a hand on her shoulder.

"Thank you." She let the tears fall.

"Bit of a shock, eh? Don't worry, I'll soon have him out of here and this place cleaned up."

"He broke the back door."

"Don't worry about it."

"I used the giraffe to hit him and—"

"I *said* don't worry about it."

At his prompting, she packed her things and loaded the car, leaving Noah until last. A black-haired man nodded to her from his SUV as she carried her son to his car seat. Clipping him in, she thrust what she'd done out of her mind and got in the driver's side, putting the location into the satnav, her hand shaking.

She drove away from the little wooden chalet, past others at the edge of a winding road, and headed towards her new destination, a changed woman. She wasn't the Becky of her younger years, wasn't the Becky who'd first met Lemon, he'd erased her, and she wasn't the woman he'd turned her into. Now, she was someone else yet again, and she had to put her trust in Orion and his 'I B 40' son to keep her safe until she could go back to London.

If she ever did.

Maybe it was better if she went somewhere else entirely.

A fresh start.

Chapter Twenty-Three

Despite The Network not being on Janine's workload, this was murder, so she stood in the tent erected around the lamppost with various other officers. Colin, beside her, mouth-breathed beneath his mask, the Darth-Vader sound getting on her tits. Cameron had followed them into work, then here, and had parked nearby but away from the site. She supposed he stood somewhere, watching for her to leave the scene. She could only hope he didn't get spotted. Being asked why he loitered could have a detrimental effect—he might become a suspect, and having to look into him could very well pull out all his skeletons, bones that really should stay hidden.

She'd received a stream of messages from the twins, likely George, and when she'd woken up after a lovely sleep, knowing Cameron was there to look out for her, the last thing she'd wanted was more hassle.

But she'd got it in the form of a dead Lemon sitting against the lamppost outside her fucking *boss'* house. George had a bloody weird sense of humour if he found this location funny, but then again, he might have chosen it so the body was seen by the relevant person sooner rather than later—a message to say: *We know who you are and what you've been doing.* Did that mean Lemon had knowledge of who was who in the organisation and had told George who the bent coppers were? Or was the DCI in the clear and the only detective the twins trusted to handle this? He hadn't said, which was frustrating.

"Who the hell *is* this bloke?" Colin muttered and pointed at Lemon.

"He's known to us. A local man who dabbles in a bit of this and that, no one we've ever been worried about to any degree."

She knew he was the assassin, but as usual, she had to wait until the clue George had left behind had been discovered. She wasn't prepared to be the one to find it. Too often in the past it had been her, and she wanted the limelight off herself. Still, she'd suggest it in a minute once Jim, the pathologist, finished his initial perusal.

"He must have got himself into some shit then if he's been killed," Colin said. He plaited his legs. "Having your cock and balls cut off…" He shuddered. "I can't even think about it. And what the fuck's happened to his *mouth*?"

Janine hadn't been furnished with the full details, it was better that she turned up here, her shock genuine. "God knows, but someone's had a good go at him. They've stapled his eyes open an' all."

Jim stood from his crouch, bending to pick up his clipboard and jotting down notes. "He had something inserted into his mouth that had the ability to stretch then split the lips and break the teeth, so we're not talking your common or garden device here. As for the penis, a clean cut, perhaps with extremely sharp scissors."

"Bloody hell," Colin mumbled.

"Indeed." Jim wrote something else. "The testicles are another matter. They've been literally ripped off with some kind of implement, but the resulting mess of gouged flesh there indicates something with sharp edges was dragged down it."

"It's put me off mince, I can tell you." Colin blinked, his eyes watering. "No more chilli for me for a while."

Jim didn't find dark humour funny in front of his patients and gave Colin a stern glare over the top of his mask. "Likening a wound to the meat you put in your dinner isn't appropriate and highly crass. Please don't talk about the dead in that way again, at least not in front of me."

Colin glanced at Janine who raised her eyebrows to say: *I told you so.*

"Okay," Jim said, "I'm happy to take a look at the back now the photos have been taken of him in situ. Can you move away so I can place him down?" He put the severed penis into a bag, labelled and boxed it, laid out a large square of plastic sheeting, and carefully moved Lemon onto it, facedown. "Ah, how curious. He has marks from the top of his back to his calves and some puncture wounds."

"And a bullet in his arse if I'm any judge," Colin said.

Jim sighed. "Yes, and a bullet in his posterior. Could you either refrain from the commentary or leave the tent, Colin? You're distracting me."

"Fine by me." Colin tromped out, ever eager to be excluded from anything work-related if he could get away with it.

The photographer in the corner snorted.

"What are the marks and punctures, Jim?" Janine asked, already knowing what they'd be.

"I'm unsure. Perhaps a device like an Iron Maiden, although I would expect there to be marks on his front, too, if it's the type of thing I'm thinking of. Hmm. Maybe he was laid on a bed of nails? I'll know more when I do a full examination. Now, the neck. I'd say thin wire. The cervical spine is intact…the head is only staying on because of that. What an utter monster, whoever did this."

Yes, George could be a monster, but oddly, Janine understood his motives. He did what other people wished they could do: teaching people a bloody hard lesson.

She shifted from foot to foot. "Can I ask you to check the clothes for me? He might have a wallet in a pocket or something. I know who he is, but seeing ID is preferable."

Jim nodded. "Photos of his back, please." He stepped out of the way of the photographer and removed his gloves, putting them in an evidence bag and pulling new ones on. He approached the clothes, feeling inside the pocket of the black trousers on the top. "No wallet that I can feel."

Janine supposed, if Lemon had been out in Minion mode, he wouldn't want to carry identification. As she'd clocked who he was visually, at least she could tell his mother.

Jim drew out a sandwich bag with a piece of paper inside. "Hmm. Rather like the Zofia Kowalczyk case, don't you think?"

"Different bag style."

Not that it made a difference. The inference was there. Stretching out her gloved hand, Janine took it from him and prepared herself for whatever had been written on it.

Meet The Network's assassin, responsible for the deaths of detectives Sykes and Mallard, among others.

"Bloody hell," she shouted to fake shock. "I've got to go and see the DCI."

She put the note bag into an evidence bag, used Jim's pen to fill out the details on it, and left the tent. She sorted fresh booties and carried the bag up her boss' front garden path. A PC stood at the door and smiled at her, allowing her inside.

"Sir?" she called.

"In here, Janine."

She entered a kitchen at the back, the DCI sitting at a table, a couple of refugee case officers in other seats.

"What's the matter?" he asked, his forehead scrunched in a frown.

While she didn't know if she could trust him or the other officers, she had to behave as she usually would. She turned the note round and held it up so they could read it.

"Jesus Christ," he muttered. "Get that logged," he told DC Garvey. "Take it directly to the lab yourself—now. I don't want anyone else knowing about it except us for the minute. I trust

285

you three, but who knows if anyone else is fucking bent on the team. Warn forensics to keep it quiet as well."

Is he saying that so I won't think it's him?

Garvey took gloves out of a box on the table and put them on. Taking the evidence from Janine, he left the room.

"So an assassin has killed the assassin," the DCI said. "Interesting. Someone out there knows more than we think."

"Do you reckon it's a disgruntled Network employee?" Janine asked.

"I don't know, but in light of the other bodies being discovered this evening, and the refugee house and those poor women, someone has a problem with the organisation apart from us."

"Um, you've lost me," Janine said; no way could she let him think she knew all about it.

"Bugger, I forgot you didn't know." He explained what had been happening, then said, "They've had a ruddy killing spree. A check is being done on incoming and outgoing flights for the past week from all destinations—de Luca didn't come up in the search, so if he's back, which is likely, seeing as another house has been found, then he's using a new name. That house tells me he was intent on starting up again, he thought enough time had passed."

"What has that got to do with this murder, though?" DC Payne asked. "There have been no Network employees murdered since Mallard."

"That we know of." The DCI rubbed his tired-looking eyes. "The last thing I expected when I nipped home for a kip after being called out to that house was to see a dead body outside mine—*my* home, which says whoever did this knows I'm overseeing the refugee team. They're trying to help, albeit in a misguided way."

Janine played dumb. "How do you know they're helping?"

"The note in the sandwich bag, the same as with Zofia Kowalczyk's body." He let out a breath. "I meant what I said earlier. I want this kept under wraps for now, so no mentioning it to anyone. Someone else could be working with us, as well as The Network. I've issued the same warning to other officers about the four men's deaths and the women, although that will be more difficult because of the amount of people who were asked to come in. If I can just buy a few hours to think out our next move…"

Or so de Luca can get away?

Janine hated this bullshit, suspecting him. He'd sounded genuine, though. What if the mole was DCs Garvey or Payne?

"So you want to me to act as if this is any other murder, sir?" she asked.

"Yes, go through the motions, but stop your team from digging too deep. Concentrate on Lemon's life outside of being an assassin. Speak to his parents, any girlfriend or wife."

"I'll go back to the station with Colin now and look up the deceased's details." She was aware of them already but had to play this as if she wasn't.

"Did he read the note? Colin, I mean."

She shook her head. "No. Jim didn't have time to either."

"Good, good. Thank you, Janine. As you can understand, this is sensitive information."

She said goodbye and left the house.

Sheila Sutton, the crime scene manager, came over. "It's my niece's ex. Lemon."

"Oh, bloody hell." Janine drew her mask down. "Do you need to step away from this one?"

"No, he's a bastard, left her with a baby not long ago. I'm okay to continue. The boss knows, and he said if I remain objective, I'm okay to stay." She blew out air, puffing up her mask. "I don't know how Becky will take it, though. She's kept herself to herself a lot since Noah was born. This might still come as a big blow. Even though he fucked off and abandoned her, there could still be feelings involved."

"Would the news be better coming from you?"

"No, stick to the usual procedure. Uniforms can have the honours, or maybe you could do it? She wouldn't want anyone in the family to see her grief until she's ready. She's private, has always kept things to herself because she doesn't want to bother anyone with her hassles. Mind you, she went through a patch of keep asking her mum and dad for money, Lemon wasn't providing his share of the rent and whatever, but like I said, she went quiet, so we all assumed she was coping."

"Okay, we'll locate her. I'd best go. We've got the next of kin to tell first."

"I don't envy you. Faith is an acquired taste."

"Thanks for the warning. Take care."

Signing out of the scene and depositing her protectives in the designated evidence bag, Janine found Colin sitting in her car. She got in and buckled up.

"What had you haring into the house like your pubes were on fire?" he asked and fished around in the door cubby for the can of Pepsi Max he'd put there when she'd picked him up.

"Christ, Colin, a fizzy pop at this time of the morning?"

"I'm thirsty. Seeing that bloke with his jewels cut off sent my mouth dry." He pulled the tab, the hiss of the bubbles being released sounding loud.

She eased away from the kerb and drove away.

"So come on, then," he said. "What's going on?"

"I shouldn't tell you."

He harrumphed. "I doubt you should have told me about the shit you've found yourself in either, but you did."

She sighed. "This goes no further, okay?"

"Of course it bloody won't."

"You know I said Lemon was nothing to worry about?"

"Yeah…"

"Jim found a note in his pocket—inside a *sandwich* bag."

"Oh."

"I know. What if it's the same person who left the note with Zofia? We've got either a pissed-off Network employee who wants to get the others in the shit, or the boss is getting rid of people who are involved, like he did before."

"What, *our* boss?"

"*No*, the one in The fucking *Network*. Wake up, Colin."

"If you used the man's name, I wouldn't get confused."

"De Luca. Happy now?" She turned a corner. "Get this. The note said *Lemon's* the bloody assassin."

"What? So why would de Luca kill his best killer?"

"I don't think he did. Someone discovered Lemon was with The Network and bumped him off."

"If it isn't a Network person, who would it be?"

She shrugged and stopped at a red light. "Maybe a copper?"

"A copper? Are you shitting me?"

"Think about it. What if it's a mole and the boss—*not* ours—wanted Lemon out of the picture in case he spilled the beans about the kills he's done? Or it could be yet another employee doing it, a new assassin. Oh, I don't fucking know, but it's doing my tree in. The DCI wants it kept quiet."

"What quiet?"

"The note! You're seriously doing my head in, mate." She spun the car in a U-turn.

"Where are you going?"

"The twenty-four-hour McDonald's to get you a coffee. You need a strong punch in the face with caffeine before I do it myself."

She went into the drive-through and ordered them both one. Back on the road, she sighed. She shouldn't take her frustration out on Colin, but God, he acted so thick at times.

She glanced in the rearview. Cameron followed them.

"Why does the DCI want it kept quiet?" Colin asked.

"I wondered when you'd catch up. Your guess is probably the same as mine. If he's in on it, he'll want to help de Luca get away."

"But wouldn't he have done that when he was called out to the new refugee house?"

A spear of suspicion prodded her. "How did you know about that?"

"A couple of PCs were talking about it when Jim kicked me out of the tent."

"He didn't kick you out, he asked you to leave because you were pissing him off. Shit, I'm going to have to let the DCI know officers are talking. He warned them all to keep quiet. Who were they?"

"I'm not dropping any names. They're only young lads."

Janine backed down. "Maybe they were both at the house and were only discussing it between them."

"It's not our problem if word spreads."

"I suppose not, but I want de Luca caught. I don't want to have to keep looking over my shoulder." She remembered the messages. George had said he'd pretended to be Lemon and had arranged a meet with what he'd called 'the head of the snake'. He planned to get de Luca's phone and leave it with him after he'd left him in a secure location, which he'd inform the police about later. If all those names rooted everyone out, she wouldn't have to be afraid anymore.

"So what are we meant to do now?" Colin asked.

"Treat Lemon's death like any other murder case."

"Doesn't he have a proper name?"

"Of course he bloody does," she snapped.

Colin sniffed. "Maybe you should use it when we visit his next of kin."

"No point. His mother calls him Lemon an' all."

"Bloody Nora." Colin took a tentative sip of his coffee. With the takeaway lid on the cup, it was likely to still be raging hot. "So we go back to the station, dig out her address, and break the news. That's usually a job for uniforms."

"I know, but I've been told to deal with it."

"Fair enough."

She pulled into the station car park. If Colin kept his divvy head on, it was going to be a long sodding day.

At five to eight, with Cameron parked down the road, Janine knocked on Lemon's mother's door. A dishevelled, hard-looking woman answered, her features chiselled, her body thin, arms folded. In a grey dressing gown and pink fluffy slippers, her short, dyed-black hair matted on one side, she narrowed her red-rimmed eyes at them.

I wouldn't want to mess with her down a dark alley.

"Yes?" she barked. "Don't tell me. You're pigs. I can smell you a mile away."

How nice, the anti-police brigade's leader. Janine smiled. "Faith Lemon?"

"Yeah?" Faith said. "And who's asking? Do I have a couple of low-level DCs on my doorstep, or have they sent someone with a bit more authority?"

Janine held her ID up. "DI Janine Sheldon. Could we come in and have a word?"

"If you're after my son, he's in bed and has been since early evening yesterday. He's not well. Got the flu or summat. Sneezing and coughing."

Janine smiled again. "I'm afraid he *isn't* in bed, Ms Lemon."

"How do *you* fucking know? Been in my house and up to his room, have you? Seen him under the covers? Or have you used one of them drones to spy on him through the window?"

Why the hell is she so pissy? "No. We're aware of where Lemon is. We've not long seen him." *Dead as a fucking doornail.*

Faith's cheeks reddened; she been caught lying, and she knew it. "Then he must have gone out while I was asleep. Probably to get some

Lemsip. Been nicked for something he hasn't done, has he? That's what you lot do, isn't it? Arrest people for no good reason?"

"He hasn't been arrested," Colin said.

Faith seemed to prefer a man speaking to her; she visibly relaxed and gave him a small smile. Maybe that was why she was so arsey, she didn't like dealing with Janine. Did she feel threatened by other women?

Colin smiled back. "We really do need to come in."

As if Faith now understood the gravity of the situation, her cheeks lost their splotches and paled. She stepped back then turned to walk down the hallway towards a kitchen where a kettle boiled on the worktop, steam billowing and leaving condensation on the window behind a potted plant.

Janine and Colin entered, Colin shutting the door. They joined her in the kitchen, Janine dreading the upcoming conversation. With Faith being so mardy, who knew how she'd take the news.

Faith filled three cups with boiled water. "I'm making tea, for the shock I reckon is coming my way."

She doesn't sound as bolshy. Maybe we've taken some of that wind out of her sails.

"I can do that for you," Colin said.

"No, I need to keep busy. Just say what you've come to say." Faith kept her back to them. To hide tears?

"Please could you sit down?" Janine asked, not wanting the woman to hurt herself if she collapsed after they delivered the blow.

Faith squeezed teabags against the inside of the cups. Janine and Colin stared at each other as she took milk out of the fridge and acted as if she were alone, no one waiting on her to take a seat. A coping mechanism, that much was obvious. She finished making the tea and took the cups over to the table, not bothering with coasters which stood in a pile at the centre. Janine went over and dealt them out, put the cups on top, then they all sat.

Faith stared at a spot on the wall behind Janine. "He's dead, isn't he? You can't tell me any different, because I felt it. I woke up, had this feeling in the pit of my stomach. Couldn't sleep afterwards."

Janine nodded. "I visually identified him at the scene."

"What scene?" Faith waggled a finger. "And I want to know everything, so no sugar-coating shit. Who, what, why, the lot. I'm his mother, I deserve to know."

No tears yet, but they would come, most likely when she was alone. Faith seemed the kind to hide her deeper emotions.

Janine took a breath. "He was discovered outside our boss' house. Naked. His private parts had been cut off." She paused to gauge whether Faith *really* wanted to know everything.

It seemed she did, as she raised her eyebrows as if to say: And?

"His throat had been sliced all the way around. He'd been shot in the backside, and his eyes were stapled open." This didn't feel right, giving her all the gory details, even though the woman had asked for them. Unprofessional. Janine moved on. "A note had been left with the body, accusing Lemon of being an assassin. Do you know anything about that?"

Faith choked on a laugh. "You what? My son, an assassin?"

"That has yet to be proved, but yes, it was stated."

Faith sighed, more air deflating from her sails. "So he's been killing people for the Sparrows, then." She came off as resigned. Disappointed.

While Janine already knew about Lemon's involvement with the gang, according to Colin, this was news, so she made out it was the same for her, too. "The Sparrows?"

Faith nodded. "Them lot from Sparrow Road. A few men, selling drugs and whatever. I knew he was hanging around with them, people talk down here, you know, but I didn't think he was into anything that would get him killed."

"Do you know their names, the other Sparrows?"

Some of Faith's mettle returned, her spine going stiff. "I'm not grassing anyone up. I don't want their old dears coming round here and accusing me of being a snitch. Believe me, when that lot down Sparrow Road get their claws in, your life isn't worth living."

Janine sipped some tea. "Don't worry, we'll find out who they are. The note indicated the assassin work wasn't for the Sparrows, though."

Faith frowned. "What? Who the hell else *could* it be?"

"Have you been following the news about The Network?"

Faith's mouth dropped open. "You what? Those fucking *sickos*?"

"Yes. Whoever wrote the note said Lemon was their assassin."

"But that would mean he killed those two blokes who were found in the river, and that Patrick from the Bassett Hound, and that kid who lived in the flat above the chippy."

"It would, yes. Four other men were killed a few hours ago as well. So *did* he go to bed early? Are you prepared to pervert the course of justice *now*?"

Faith's shoulders drooped. "You know, normally I'd swear blind he was with me, but he hasn't been right lately, and I should have known he was up to something. I've always stood up for him, even acting a right cow to his ex because I wanted him to know I was on his side, I wanted him to love me for it, but this?" She bit her lip. Had a thought. "Oh God, Becky... His ex, the mother of his child."

"We looked up her address before we came here; I assume that's where Lemon lived previously? He's still down on record as residing there."

"Yeah, I haven't got round to telling any bill people he's here now, for the council tax an' that."

"Okay, we'll go there after. When did you last see your son?"

"Before I went to work yesterday, late morning."

"And how did he seem?"

"Calm, which was odd, because he's been snappy, biting my head off more often than not. I put it down to Becky getting on his case, asking for money and the like. She came here, you know, and I sent her away with a flea in her ear. Maybe I shouldn't have done that, but I was jealous of her. She took my son away from me for a while."

"Do you regret sending her away?"

"I do now! Noah…he's all I've got left of my boy. What if she doesn't let me see him?"

"Then it's time to apologise, build bridges," Colin said.

They chatted for a while longer, then Faith got hold of the next-door neighbour to come and sit with her for a bit. With the promise that Faith would go in and do the formal identification once the post-mortem had been completed, Janine and

Colin left, going straight to Becky's. Janine was aware she wasn't in, taking a break in Southend until the twins had sorted Lemon, but she had to pretend otherwise.

She knocked on the door several times, Colin sighing at getting no response. A creak of hinges drew Janine's attention to the house on the right.

"She went off yesterday with bags and a suitcase," the elderly woman said, hair coated in a blue rinse, her flowery apron giving the impression of a true British old lady.

"And you are?" Janine held up her ID.

"Mrs Urwin." She came out, pulling the door to. "I don't want to wake my husband…"

Janine detected fear there. "Is everything okay at home?"

"Nothing I'm not used to. It's been years so… Anyway, you don't want to talk about me."

Janine took a card out of her pocket and handed it over. "If you ever need help…"

Mrs Urwin took it and slipped it in her apron pocket. "What's Becky done?"

"Nothing, we just need a chat."

"Then it's that man of hers you'll be wanting to talk about, no doubt. He hasn't lived here for a good couple of months now. A bully, that's what he is. I heard plenty through the walls."

"Do you know where she went?"

"No, but like I said, she had a suitcase, so maybe she went on a little holiday or moved out?"

"Thank you, that's very helpful."

Janine said goodbye, and she got in the car, waiting for Colin to do up his seat belt.

"I'll get on with looking for her when we get back to the station," he said.

"Thanks."

"Do we leave her to finish her holiday or what?"

"No. She might not be the NOK, but that baby's father is dead, so she has a right to know. Once we establish where she is via ANPR and that she didn't come back to kill Lemon, and if we find out where she's staying, officers can drop by and speak to her."

Janine drove away, pleased with how things had turned out. Mrs Urwin had provided the information they needed, which saved Janine having a fake eureka moment in locating Becky by suggesting she might have gone off for a break. Now she had the pointless task of poking into Lemon's life and finding the people in the Sparrow gang.

People who were now all dead bar one, not that anyone else at the station knew that.

Where are you, Vanga?

At ten-twenty, Cameron likely sitting in his car opposite the station, Janine received belated information from George. Becky had accidentally killed Vanga who currently resided in a big chest freezer at some bloke's lock-up in Southend until he could be disposed of in darkness. Orion, a friend of the twins, had stepped in to clean up Becky's mess. She was now spending the rest of her holiday in one of Orion's caravans. Janine prayed the woman wouldn't let anything slip when the police visited her about Lemon. Surely George and Greg would have briefed her on what to say and how to act, wouldn't they?

Janine left the toilet, her burner on vibrate in her pocket. She marched down the corridor, on her way to seeing how much information Colin had dredged up about Becky's whereabouts, Lemon's non-Network activities, and the names of the Sparrow members. Head down, lost in thought, she was brought up short when she bumped into someone. She raised her head, about to apologise, and the blood seemed to drain out of her.

"What are you doing here?" she asked.

"I've been drafted to help with The Network case."

"Oh, was that today? Only, I haven't seen you around."

"No, it's been a while. I'm holed up in an office mainly, doing searches. Can we have a chat?"

Her stomach lurched. She didn't want to have a conversation about The Network; she needed to put as much distance as she could between herself and the investigation. While one assassin had been murdered, there was bound to be another who'd finish what Lemon had started. Maybe this 'chat' would shed some light on who that might be.

"What about?" she asked.

"I've got some advice for you."

She frowned. "We'll go to my office, then."

"No, somewhere else. Meet me in the café down the road in ten minutes."

She watched the officer walk away and asked herself a million questions, the main ones being: Why were they assigned to the refugee case? Did they apply, suggested by de Luca, or were they drafted like they'd said? Had she just been talking to the mole? That didn't make sense. They were a stickler for the rules, but could that just be a front so they weren't suspected? And what was this advice?

She had a horrible feeling she knew the answer to that. She wasn't dead—yet—and maybe she'd be allowed to live if she gave them the right answers.

She stopped by the incident room and told the team she'd be back in half an hour. Then she went into her office, closed the door and the blinds, and messaged Cameron.

JANINE: I SUSPECT I'M ABOUT TO BE GIVEN A WARNING FROM THE NETWORK. GOING TO THE CAFÉ DOWN THE ROAD NOW. PLEASE COME INSIDE AND SIT CLOSE ENOUGH TO HEAR, BUT I DON'T KNOW IF THEY KNOW YOUR FACE, THEY COULD HAVE BEEN WATCHING YOU FOLLOWING ME, SO HAVE YOU GOT A DISGUISE LIKE GG USES?

CAMERON: I COULD PUT SOME GLASSES AND A CAP ON, BUT THAT'S ABOUT IT. I'VE ALREADY GOT A BEARD.

JANINE: THAT'LL HAVE TO DO. IF THEY'RE WHO I THINK THEY ARE, THEN I HAVE A CHOICE TO MAKE. LET GG DEAL WITH THEM, OR TELL A SENIOR OFFICER. I'LL GIVE YOU A HEADS-UP IF THEY'RE ANYONE TO WORRY ABOUT AS THEY MAY NEED TO BE WATCHED, AND IT WON'T DO ANY HARM FOR YOU TO KNOW WHO THEY ARE IN CASE WE GET A VISIT TONIGHT IF I DON'T GRASS THEM UP—GG MIGHT WANT TO TAKE OVER WHAT HAPPENS TO THEM.

CAMERON: OKAY.

She added the description of the person she'd be meeting, then left the station. The walk to the café had an ominous quality to it, and she shivered, glancing over her shoulder to check if she was being followed. She stopped at the café door, nosed inside, and spotted them at a table in the far corner, others empty beside it. Hoping Cameron didn't sit *that* close, she joined the person at the table, ignoring the cup of coffee they'd bought for her. She didn't trust that something hadn't been put in it. Of course, this could all be her imagination, this whole scenario an innocent meeting where they needed to pass on a message from the DCI or something.

"Okay, shoot," she said.

They stared at her, head cocked. "What I'm about to tell you...I'll deny every word, and you'll be in the shit for it, do you understand?"

She understood all right. Hadn't she said similar to Colin? "Fair enough. So you're letting me know if I leave here and blab to anyone, I'll pay for it. Lovely."

"Still sarcastic, I see. That chip on your shoulder must really weigh you down. But your summary is about right. I'm not fucking around here, Janine. This is serious business. I'm giving you a warning which may actually save your life if you play ball."

So they *were* from The Network, then. No big surprise. She should know by now to trust her instincts.

Out of the corner of her eye, she spied Cameron sitting to her left, holding up a newspaper.

"Come on then, give it to me." She folded her arms.

They leant forward and said quietly, "I wanted to give you a chance to continue living, because you could be useful. I hold sway, and my boss will listen to me."

Now she knew how Colin had felt when she'd used the term 'boss'. "Which boss?"

"Work it out."

"So you're with The Network."

They sat back, smug. "Bet you didn't see *that* one coming, did you?"

"So what are you proposing, that I come over to the dark side with you?"

"That's the only option."

But not one she'd ever agree to, unless she got permission to find out information then pass it back to the refugee team. "So you know there was a hit out on me last night and it failed?"

"How did you know about that?"

She tapped the side of her nose.

They shook their head. "Obviously it didn't happen, else you wouldn't be sitting here. It didn't fail; the person who was sent to kill you had other things to do. Deleting a few men and relocating some women."

She smiled. "You don't even know what else has happened, do you?"

A frown. "Of course I do, I just bloody told you."

"No, *after* the murders and relocation."

Unsure and on the back foot, they scratched their head.

They don't know about Lemon. "Looks like we're on different pages—the page I'm on, you might not be privy to."

"What do you mean?"

"There's been a blackout. A need-to-know basis put in place. Some people in the refugee team are in the know, but not all. *Clearly.*"

"What the fuck are you on about?"

"Sorry, my orders were to keep it to myself." She smirked. "So is that all, or do you have more advice for me?"

"I was going to tell the boss to bring you into the fold, but I've changed my mind. Unless you're willing to let me in on what's being blacked out."

"I value my job, so no."

"Then Lemon will kill you."

"Really?"

"What?"

She had to keep them talking until after eleven o'clock, when George was meeting de Luca, to prevent any messages tipping him off. "Listen, I don't know how far into this you are, whether you sampled refugees or what, and how long you've been up to your neck in this, but I thought better of you than that. You're a good actor, I'll give you that much, because I didn't suspect a thing, but now I look back on it, yes, I can see it was you. Things are about to change, and no matter how well you think you've covered your tracks, your involvement will be uncovered eventually. You're a police officer. You know how it works."

"I can easily erase information using someone else's login details."

"But you can't erase it from officers' heads, can you. If anyone notes the info has been deleted, they'll just put it back. Are you the only bent copper left for The Network in London?"

They nodded. "The other two were novices. Deserved to die."

"If I were you, I'd duck out of any Network business now, because after this latest debacle, shit's going to get real."

A fleeting expression, one of concern, then it was gone. "Why warn me?"

"Because you're good at your job and you're of better use in the force, not in the nick." This was true, but she'd only said it to stall them, to give them pause after this meeting so she had time to decide what to do. "If you're thinking of messaging or phoning de Luca, my advice? Don't. Seriously, *don't*. Get rid of any phones, any links. Make yourself appear clean, for fuck's sake."

"This is your way of telling me crap is about to explode on a whole new level. It's related to the blackout information."

"Give yourself a gold star. Now, I have to go. I need to get back to my murder investigation."

"Fair's fair—if you're helping me, I'll tell de Luca you're not a threat."

She shrugged. "Your call, but to be honest, I'm *not* a threat. I'm not involved with The Network case and don't want to be. If you're intent on staying with de Luca, you know who really needs taking out."

"The DCI?"

"He won't stop until this is wrapped up, until he's found everyone."

"Thanks. Seems I've got a lot to think about."

"You do."

They got up. Stared down at her. "Good luck."

"Same to you. You're going to fucking need it."

She remained where she was for two minutes, then glanced at Cameron who peeped at her over the top of the newspaper. She sent him a message.

JANINE: I'VE MADE A DECISION. I'M GOING TO TAKE THIS HIGHER. WILL WALK TO THE PUBLIC LOOS DOWN THE ROAD. COVER ME.

CAMERON: SOMEONE'S ALREADY TAILING YOUR 'GUEST'. I LET GG KNOW WHAT'S GOING ON.

JANINE: THANKS.

At least she didn't have that to worry about.

She left the café, walking to the toilets. Twenty pence inserted in the slot, she entered and checked each cubicle. With no one there, she rang her boss.

"Everything all right?" he asked.

"I've found the mole."

"What?"

"The mole on the refugee team. They just asked to meet me in a café and issued threats. Apparently, Lemon was supposed to kill me last night because I'm seen as a problem."

"Jesus Christ! Why?"

"Because I was on the original refugee team. I have a feeling everyone who worked on it is a target, including those on the new team. We *have* to find de Luca before another one of us gets a bullet in our heads."

"Shit. *Shit*! Who's the mole?"

She took a deep breath and thought of the person who had given her many a heart attack by creeping up on her, watching her every move. "DS Radburn Linton, sir."

Chapter Twenty-Four

De Luca stared at the woman he'd had delivered from the Essex house which had been closed, like all the others around the world, since the refugee case had hit the news. The bitches hadn't lost their touch in bed, though, as the men looking after them had still been taking what they wanted to keep the ladies in prime sexual condition. Waste not, want not.

Lemon deserved her as a treat, a non-monetary bonus. The man had worked diligently and professionally the whole time he'd been in The Network's employ, and after his magnificent behaviour during the night, the downtime was most likely welcome. De Luca had a suite, so Lemon could go into the second bedroom and use her to his heart's content. The suites were soundproofed, so no worries about her screams being heard. She was a high-level slut, one well used to having sex with strangers, so if she complained, she'd be reprimanded. A slap or two wouldn't go amiss, and once she went back to the house, a beating would put her back in her place.

She stared back at him from an armchair, and if he wasn't mistaken, she seemed relieved to be away from the Essex house. Perhaps she wasn't happy being locked inside for so long, and getting in bed with Lemon could be seen as something to relieve the boredom. She might feel smug at being chosen to come here, giving her a sense of self-importance that she was deemed better than the others. In reality, de Luca had given instructions for any of them to be brought here, it didn't matter who. They all had useful holes.

He didn't care *what* she felt, to be honest, so long as she performed. Soon, he'd give the go-ahead for the houses to reopen, the Users allowed to come forward and sample or purchase, but maybe he'd hold off for a while longer, especially given what Radburn might let him know regarding the outcome of Lemon's last kills. It would be obvious to the police, when the men's bodies were discovered, that this was linked, considering Mr Johnson had held the first sex party at his home and the authorities were well aware of that.

Those four men had betrayed de Luca, betrayed everyone who devoted their lives to a good cause, giving people untold pleasure via the refugees. Not many could say they were allowed to act out their fantasies without judgement. De Luca gave them the freedom to do that.

He checked his watch. Lemon would be here shortly, and de Luca could question him as to why the men who'd transported the four women hadn't sent a message to confirm they'd completed their task.

Should I be worried?

317

No, they might have gone to bed, be sleeping the morning away, forgetting to contact him — they'd be docked wages and chastised for that — but Lemon would have used his initiative and visited their homes this morning to get a response, and as he was on his way here, he likely wanted to pass on the news in person.

"Who is coming?" the woman asked, her Ukrainian accent strong.

She reminded de Luca of Mamma, the bitch who'd ruined everything. Resisting the urge to punch her face, taking all of his unresolved mother issues out on her, he inhaled through his nose and counted to ten.

"It doesn't matter who's coming," he snapped. "It's none of your concern. You're paid to fuck, nothing more. Don't go getting ideas above your station."

"When will we be going back to work properly?"

He didn't like her asking questions after he'd basically warned her to keep her mouth shut, so he gave her one of his glares. "Be quiet. You should be seen and not heard — unless you're screaming in pain."

She shrivelled at that, drawing her legs up, her feet planted on the edge of the chair. She hugged her knees and shivered, eyes wide, her bottom lip quivering.

How easy it was to scare them. To show them who was boss.

He looked at his watch again.

Eleven o'clock.

All of his questions would be answered soon.

At eleven a.m. on the dot., George waited outside de Luca's hotel suite, situated next to the corridor doorway that led to the stairs and the landing where the lifts were. Greg stood on the landing to stop anyone getting off the lift and going down the corridor, and Ichabod remained at the bottom of the stairs in case people chose that way as their route to potentially fuck this up. Everyone had put on a disguise so they all looked like Ruffian, and anyone wondering who they were could go and do one. George had paid the receptionist to turn the other way, and he needed this to go off without a hitch.

Bracing himself for possibly having to get shirty, maybe even trigger-happy, he shrugged his backpack into a more comfortable position, took a deep breath, and knocked. He'd already thought about de Luca having someone else in the room with him—not just the woman 'Lemon' had requested but a bodyguard—and he held his gun behind his back, ready for if he needed to whip it out.

A *beep* sounded, then the door opened, a man in a suit standing there but looking back into the room, perhaps ensuring the woman didn't rush up behind him in an attempt to escape. Perfect. What a twat, though, to put his faith in it being Lemon who'd arrived.

You'd think he'd be more careful, considering who he is and that the police are after him.

George shoved the arm closest to him, and the grey-haired man staggered inside, letting out an *oomph* of surprise, looking over his shoulder at who'd had the audacity to push him like that. George followed, gun up and aimed, and the fella righted himself and turned fully to stare at him.

George let the door close behind him.

"Why are you here?" De Luca breathed heavily, eyes darting about.

From the description Janine had given him, George thought he'd got the wrong man. De Luca was supposed to be black-haired, dark eyes. This geezer was nothing like what he'd imagined in his head. So *was* there a bodyguard here? If so, where was de Luca? In another room? Or had he gone out? No. When they'd watched the comings and goings outside before coming upstairs, no Italian-looking men had left.

Fucking stupid of us to think he wouldn't be in disguise.

"De Luca?" George asked, Scottish accent thick.

A flinch of the eyelids gave him his answer.

George laughed. "Did you use Just for Men or what? I thought that was to get *rid* of grey, not fucking dye your hair like it."

"I don't know what you are talking about."

"It doesn't matter."

De Luca raised his hand.

"Don't do anything silly, there's a good boy," George said. As he'd be allowing de Luca to live so the police could question him, he didn't intend to shoot him in the head like his Mad side urged him to do, getting blood all over that silver hair and beard. But a foot, a leg…maybe.

"Who the hell do you think you are?" de Luca asked.

"I'm the man who's come to cut off the head of the snake." George advanced.

De Luca reversed, moving towards the woman. Ah, he was going to use her as a human shield. Made sense, seeing as he didn't give a single shite about any of the women's welfare, only his own. The man didn't care who he hurt along the way.

As predicted, de Luca grabbed her arm and yanked her out of the chair, swinging her to stand half in front of him. He held her around the waist, his other hand over her mouth. His gun, on the bedside cabinet, was too far away for him to reach, and in the absence of another weapon, he used his thumb beneath her nostrils to cut off her air supply.

What a cock.

"Get out or she is dead," the Italian said.

"I don't think so." George pulled the trigger, the bullet entering de Luca's shin.

The impact had the desired effect. De Luca let the woman go, stumbling backwards and sitting on the bed in stunned shock. She raced towards George, which was odd, considering he could be here to kidnap her. Or did she sense he was here to save her?

"Do you understand English?" George asked.

She gripped his arm. "Yes. Please, do not hurt me."

"Go out of this room." George trained his gun on de Luca. "There's a man who looks like me on the other side of a glass door. Stay with him. When I've finished in here, we'll take you to the police."

"No," she said. "I do not have visa."

"It doesn't matter. You won't get in trouble. Now get out."

He waited for her to exit, the door closing behind her.

"You'll pay for this," de Luca said.

"You sound like you've been given a bad line in a film, mate."

"Who sent you? What have you done with my man?"

"Oh, give over with the questions. All you need to know is you've been caught, dickhead, simple as that." George gestured to de Luca's leg with his free hand. "That blood's wrecking your lovely grey trousers. Shame. Mind you, you won't need a suit where you're going. I reckon you'd look shit in trackie bottoms and a sweatshirt. Still, it's about time you were brought down to scum level."

"What do you want? I have money."

"So do I. What's more beneficial to me is a list of your employees and all the customers—and I don't just mean in London. I'm talking worldwide."

"Impossible." The bloke gasped, his face breaking out in a sweat and turning red.

"How is it impossible? You must have them on a phone, a laptop."

De Luca let out a long whine.

George found that amusing. "Is the pain really kicking in now? Here, let me give you something to take your mind off it."

He shot his other leg.

The howl of agony had George smiling wide, especially as this 'gentleman' no longer appeared in control. His suave good looks crumpled, eyes watering, and he gritted his obviously veneered teeth.

"You'll crack those fuckers if you're not careful," George said.

"Crack…what?"

"Your Hamstead Heath."

"What?"

"Your *teeth*. Fuck me, I'd have thought you'd be well up to date with the lingo, seeing as you've spent a lot of time here, but obviously not."

"You're here to talk about my *teeth*? To taunt me?"

"Nah. I've got some news for you. Lemon's dead."

De Luca clenched his hands together in a double fist. "Who?"

"Playing that game, are we? He's the bloke you sent out to kill people. Only, *I* killed *him*. But not before he squealed." A few lies wouldn't go amiss here. "I know all I need to know about your organisation. It's amazing what you can get out of someone strapped to a spiked rack. Even more amazing when you rip their bollocks off. You know how it goes. It's not like you're a stranger to violence, is it."

De Luca glanced behind him, to the gun on the other side of the bed.

"I'd shoot you before you even reached it," George said. "I wouldn't even waste my time if I were you. I could, of course, shoot both your hands, so even if you *did* manage to get your mitts on that gun, you'd have a hard time holding it.

Let's stop being a prick, shall we, and tell me where the information is."

"Why, so you can take over my world?"

"Nah, so it saves the police the job of finding it. I want all those women saved."

"No, you cannot do that. I will not allow it."

"You're in no position to allow anything, sunshine. You're pissing blood all over the carpet. Well, if you don't want to give it up voluntarily, I'm sure the coppers are competent enough to follow the trail. They can check CCTV for your face, get hold of the airport and find out which flight you took. Find out where you live now with the help of the police abroad. You had a good run, but it's over."

He shot him in the arm. De Luca screamed.

George waited for him to shut up mithering. "Hopefully you'll have a change of heart when the pigs turn up." He holstered his gun and swung his backpack off. He took out a set of mean-looking manacles linked by a thick chain and held them up. "Sorry to be cliché, my old son, but I'm attaching you to that radiator."

George belly laughed and got to work.

De Luca's phone, gun, laptop, and everything else he owned had been placed on the other side of the room. Whoever had just been in here was a madman—and he would have been a great asset for The Network had de Luca met him in another time, another place. The red-haired bastard must have been tipped off by someone in the organisation to have known who Lemon was. Who had done that?

Not knowing created acid in de Luca's gullet, and it zipped up to burn the back of his throat, sour and sharp. It had come to this degradation, being chained to a radiator, waiting for whatever came next. He hadn't opted for his suite to be cleaned during his stay, so even a maid wouldn't come by to rescue him. With no other appointments booked for today, he couldn't even be freed by a client coming to discuss the sale of women.

Opting for a soundproofed room didn't seem so clever now. No one would have heard those gunshots. What sort of man was the redhead to not have been bothered about that? No one would have assumed the rooms let out no sound unless they'd stayed here.

The pain in de Luca's legs and arm roared, and he clenched his teeth, scrunching his eyes shut. How long would he be left here? Would that man tell the police straight away or leave him to bleed for a while longer? And sitting on the floor—the ultimate humiliation.

The bleep of a card going into the door slot had him staring down the short hallway, his heart rate going haywire, his tongue losing all saliva. The door swung open, the handle bashing into the wall.

"Police! Put down any weapons!"

Men entered, all in black, helmets on, visors shielding their faces.

And guns. An armed response unit.

Despite the pain, de Luca smiled at that. So much fuss for him, just one man who'd worked right under their noses for so long, luring women into the country and letting people do whatever they liked with them.

Papà would be so proud of how important he was.

The first call had been made when Janine was still in her office, although she'd gleaned information about it as a second call had come in to the main desk while she'd been passing on her way to the vending machine. ARU had been sent to a Shoreditch hotel to collect de Luca, so George and Greg had come up trumps. The sergeant on duty, Nigel, had called out to Janine to pass on that not only had The Network boss been shot and chained to a radiator, but a refugee had been rescued and currently sat in the Lamb and Flag down the road, just past the public toilets, an anonymous Scottish male reporting it.

Without thinking, Janine rushed out of the station and ran to the pub, assuming Cameron would follow. She hadn't had any messages from the twins, which was just as well, because she'd been shocked and pleased when Nigel had informed her about de Luca and the woman, the reaction required to keep any suspicion off her.

She pushed through the double doors and spotted her ahead immediately—the skimpy red dress and excessive eye makeup was a dead giveaway, plus the haunted look in her eyes. Sitting in a corner, a glass of Coke and a half-eaten baguette on the table in front of her, she pensively stared at Janine, her expression one of: Should I bolt?

Janine held both hands up and approached, giving her a smile to show she wasn't a threat. She took her ID out and held it up, gaining glances from other customers who turned to watch, probably thinking she'd be making an arrest any second. Some had phones out. *Shit.* Once she was at the table, she sat slowly with her back to those taking photos or filming, not wanting to spook her. "I'm a police officer. I understand you need some help."

The woman nodded.

"What's your name?" Janine asked quietly.

"Veronika Chumak. I am from Ukraine."

"Who brought you here?"

"Men with red hair and beards. Three of them. They were nice to me. Bought me food and drink." She gestured to the table.

"Did they say anything much to you?" Janine, aware George liked to throw promises around that she might not be able to keep, had to know the score.

"Only that I would be safe now. I might be able to stay here."

Thank God he didn't make any grand gestures. "I'll arrange that for you. When you've finished your food, we'll nip to the station. I'll take a statement, and then we can go from there, all right?"

"My family…"

"We'll try to find them, let them know you're okay."

"What is happening with the war? Is it over?"

Jesus, to think this poor woman had been kept away from the news all this time. Of course, with no new refugees coming in, there was no one to pass on any news.

Janine shook her head. "Sadly, no. I'm sorry."

Tears filled Veronika's eyes. "I hope my mother and father are not dead."

So do I, love. Christ, this is hard.

Once again, she'd make sure she was the one to see Veronika through the relocation process from start to finish, like she had with Oleksiy and Bohuslava. It would hopefully be her last link to The Network in her job. After that, she wanted nothing more to do with it.

She just had to pray no other assassin had been briefed to kill her—and got to her before they were all apprehended.

In their usual clothes and minus the red wigs and beards, George, Greg, and Ichabod sat in the Taj for their celebratory meal, a slap-up lunch George was sorely in need of. He'd left Veronika sitting in the Lamb and Flag but had hung around in his Ruffian disguise, waiting for officers to turn up, happy to see it had been Janine.

While he'd been attaching de Luca to the radiator, he'd at least got some information out of him regarding the names of all the people in his employ. Suddenly, the man had decided he wanted to take everyone else down with him and revealed the code to open a hidden file on his laptop, although he'd warned the code would need deciphering.

"That's all right, I've got a translation app on Lemon's phone," George had said. "Bit of a stupid move on your part, getting an app created, but whatever. I suppose you thought you were untouchable. Prick."

He'd passed that info to the police from a backstreet location, then dumped the SIM, driving away to drop Veronika off. He had the gun to get rid of an' all, but that could come later. For now, he wanted his belly filled.

"Poor feckin' cow," Ichabod muttered.

Like George, he'd obviously been thinking of Veronika.

"Do ye think it's all over now?" Ichabod poked a fork into a big onion bhaji and took a bite, the crunch loud.

"We can only hope," Greg said. "We've done our part, now it's up to the police."

"I'm still worried about Janine, though," George said.

Greg nodded. "Cameron can stick with her for the time being, until we know everyone's been caught."

"That could take a while." Ichabod dipped his bhaji in his curry sauce. "I mean, a lot of them have already gone tae ground from before. Covered their arses. Maybe changed their names."

George shrugged. "Then Cameron will be attached to Janine's hip for the rest of her life."

Greg laughed. "She won't like that."

George smiled. "Tough. She'll come round once she realises it's for her own good."

Quietly, so no diners overheard, they went through their movements since Becky had dropped the bombshell about Lemon, going over alibis. Who'd have thought it would open up such a big can of worms. Still, The Network would be no more, providing de Luca hadn't left instructions for someone else to take over, someone who'd dish out new identities to people before the coppers could catch up with them.

He'd be in hospital now, getting those bullets taken out of him.

I hope it hurts.

"I wonder if he'll talk more once he's in a police interview," George said.

"De Luca?" Greg broke his naan in half. "Maybe. What did you get a sense of when you spoke to him?"

"Arrogant at first, then he soon shat himself."

"A gun will do that." Ichabod sipped some lager. "I don't know about ye, but I'm lookin' forward tae me bed."

"You and me both," Greg said.

George put his fork down. "Hang on, you had some kip during the night, bruv. It was *me* who stayed up and kept an eye on things."

Greg flicked George's nose. "Shut your face, Moaning Mini."

George was about to retort and flick him the fuck back, but his phone buzzed and, much as he loved Cardigan work, he sighed. He needed a breather for an hour or so. Still, he glanced at the screen.

BECKY: CHECKING IN. I'M OKAY. ORION'S SON IS LOOKING AFTER ME.

GG: GOOD. LEMON WAS INTO MORE THAN THE SPARROWS. WILL UPDATE YOU LATER IN A PHONE CALL, WHEN LISTENING EARS AREN'T AROUND.

BECKY: OKAY.

GG: FORGET ABOUT IT FOR NOW. GO AND ENJOY THE REST OF YOUR DAY.

BECKY: I'LL TRY, CONSIDERING WHAT YOU JUST TOLD ME — AND WHAT HAPPENED TO ME DURING THE NIGHT.

GG: GIVE IT A GO, THOUGH, EH?

He slipped the phone in his pocket and chastised himself for being too blunt, considering she was probably dealing with the fact she was a killer now. He made a mental note to give her all the details if she wanted them. If she didn't, he wouldn't blame her. What Lemon had got up to wasn't for the faint of heart.

The thing was, George wasn't sure Becky could handle it.

Or had he underestimated her?

Chapter Twenty-Five

B ecky sat with I B 40 on a promenade bench in front of the sea, Noah asleep in the pushchair. It was weird how it *wasn't* weird that she sat with someone she'd not long met—*and* felt at ease with him. Instead of letting him follow her around, she'd asked him to join her, so he could sit and have lunch with her. The least she could do, seeing as he might not have wanted the job of looking after a killer while his father disposed of the body.

Maybe he's used to that sort of thing.

"You shouldn't feel bad, you know," he said, giving her an elbow nudge.

She sniffed. "I'm guessing you mean about last night."

"Yeah."

"It's hard not to feel bad." She whispered, "It's not every day you kill someone, is it."

"Err, you're talking to the wrong person."

"Oh. You do that?" Why didn't she recoil? Why had she gone so crazy at Lemon when he'd revealed some of what he'd got up to, yet with this bloke, it seemed different?

Because I thought I loved Lemon.

I B 40 leant in to say, "Only when I have to. Dad's the main killer in our family."

"You say that like it's normal."

"It is for me." He chuckled at her horrified expression. "We're no different to The Brothers, keeping this place in order, so no need to shit yourself. I won't hurt *you*."

"I'm not shitting myself. Oddly."

"That's got to be my wholesome charm working its magic, making you feel at ease."

Was he serious? She checked his face. *Ah, he's bloody joking.* "I was going to say, wholesome is *not* how I'd describe you." She sighed. Sobered. Needed someone to talk to. "There's more, not just last night."

"There usually is for the people who use Dad's chalet. No one goes there for shits and giggles. So what's going on?"

"My ex has been killed."

"He probably deserved it if it was the twins who did it. They don't just off people willy-nilly."

"Depends what he did to deserve it, but yes, you're right. If they got rid of him, it must have been bad, worse than him just treating me like shit and selling a few wraps for a gang."

He stiffened. Clenched his fists. "Treating you like shit is enough reason in my book."

She turned to him and smiled sadly. He didn't look forty, maybe thirty-five, and he had kind eyes and spoke gently, although she had a feeling, if her care had been entrusted to him, that he could get nasty in a heartbeat in order to protect her. But she didn't get the sense he was a bastard to women. Over lunch, he'd been a gentleman, pouring her Coke into a glass for her, sitting Noah on his lap when he'd woken up, saying Becky needed to eat her food in peace for once, that his mother had always dropped what she was doing for her kids. As he'd got older, he'd seen how much she'd put herself last, and he didn't like it. Felt guilty about it, being a part of it, taking her for granted. He had a bugbear with his father over it because he'd been the one to dismiss his wife as if she were the hired help. I B 40 reckoned women needed to be treated right, not used, and it wasn't any wonder his mum had waited until her son had grown, then left her husband to go and live in a cottage all by herself on the cliffs of Dover.

They're just words, and anyone could say them. He might not mean what he said.

Would that little warning voice always be there now because of Lemon?

Then it struck her. She sat on a bench with a virtual stranger. Relied on him to keep her safe, and yet... "I don't even know your name. I've been thinking of you as I B 40."

"Ah, the number plate. There's a story there."

"Want to share it?"

"Can do. Now it doesn't hurt so much."

She thought of Lemon again. He never seemed to hurt. Like he didn't carry a sympathy gene, even for himself, growing up with a nasty piece of work for a mother like Faith.

"Only if you're sure," she said.

"It's all right. Best to get these things out in the open. If you let them fester, they hurt more. They fuck with the old noggin."

Was that some sage advice? Was he warning her not to stay inside her head when it came to Lemon and Vanga? And the Mr Tomlinson thing?

He sighed. "I had this mate. We'd grown up together. Always said by the time we were forty we'd be millionaires, living the high life. Only he didn't even make it to twenty-one. Leukaemia. He told me just before he died that if I made it to forty and got rich, I needed to shout about it and live his life for him an' all. So I did. Got the number plate. Not everyone has the privilege of growing old, and I'm fucking proud I made my first million eight years after he died by working for my dad. I swear my mate's up there and made it happen."

"Maybe he is."

"My dad just thinks I'm a dickhead, telling the world my age, but it's significant, know what I mean?"

"Hmm."

"You've got to take life by the balls, Becky. Don't let it slip past you."

"I'll try."

"Try hard, because tomorrow isn't promised."

This had the potential to slip into maudlin territory, and she didn't need that. If she allowed herself to seep into the depression of knowing she was a killer, she might not ever climb back out of that deep well. "Anyway, what *is* your name?"

He laughed. "I'm Vernon. Don't say a word. It's a shit name. I don't know what my parents were thinking."

"Vern is all right, though."

He shrugged. "Marginally better."

She stared out at the beach. People sunbathed, others played ball games, and a crowd paddled in the waves. Someone zipped by in the distance on a jet ski. Did they have problems, too? Had they come here to run away from their lives, force it out of their minds for their holiday? Just thinking about how she felt in London, stifled, skint, a burden, compared to how she felt here had her re-evaluating her previous decisions. Was this only holiday fever, though? If she lived here, would real life intrude in the end? Yes, it had butted in already, what with Vanga doing what he had then dying, and George telling her Lemon was dead, but still, a measure of peace floated inside her, as if this was where she belonged.

"I don't want to go back," she said.

"Then don't."

She looked at Vernon. "It isn't that simple."

"It is if you want it to be."

"But I have nowhere to live and can't just up sticks. I'd need to find a job."

"You can do whatever you like if you put your mind to it. If you want it enough, you'll find a way. Do you want to go through the rest of your life putting up roadblocks, self-sabotaging potential happiness?"

"No, I've done enough of that."

"Well then. Besides, accommodation is sorted. I've got a big house I'm rattling around in…"

"Behave. How do I know you're not like my ex? Charming now, monster later."

"Because my dad would cut my dick off if I ever hurt a woman—bit of a hypocrite because he hurt my mum, but he's a 'do as I say, not as I do' kind of fella. If you don't want to kip at my place, Dad will lend you a caravan until you get yourself sorted."

"I'd have to pay rent."

"Maybe."

"What do you mean by that?"

"I could pay it for you. A loan, before you get up in arms and all indignant."

"But I don't even know you that well."

"So?"

His kindness touched her, but who the hell offered so much if they weren't getting anything in return?

He said he's like The Brothers, him and his dad. If I lived here, it'd be the same as me asking the twins for a loan.

"Have you had many relationships in the past?" she asked.

"A couple of longish ones—long for me anyway, which equates to a year or so—and a few short ones. Nothing to write home about."

"Why did they end?"

"One of them was just after my money. The others, they didn't want to settle down and have kids yet. I did."

"You sound like a dream man."

"Obviously not, considering they fucked off."

A little boy ran past and dropped his ice cream. His face scrunched up before the tears came, then he wailed at the sight of his scuffed knee. Vernon got up and went to the nearby ice cream van while the mother crouched to console her son. Noah woke from the racket, looked around, then dozed back off again. Vernon returned with a double 99, two Flakes sticking out, raspberry sauce dribbling.

"Oh," the mother said. "Thank you."

The boy took the ice cream and smiled, the gaps in his teeth numerous. The mum and child walked off, and Vernon sat beside Becky.

"That was a nice thing to do," she said.

"It was the *only* thing to do."

She thought about that, how sincere he'd sounded when he'd said it.

She could get used to a man like him.

"*What?*" she said, eyes wide at George's face on her phone screen.

"I said, I ripped his bollocks off and —"

She paced the caravan, Vernon sitting outside in his car so she could have privacy during the call. "I heard you the first time."

"Then why say 'what'?"

She shook her head. "Forget it. So what did he do other than be with the Sparrows?"

"I'm not sure you should be told just yet, but then again, it's going to hit the news later down the line once certain people have been rounded up. I've spoken to Janine, and she said there's a blackout on announcing what he was really up to. For now, it's just your average murder inquiry."

"Okay. Get it over with and tell me, please."

He explained about The Network.

"No…" She blinked. "I mean, Lemon, a killer? Like, a *proper* killer?"

"An assassin, if you want the right term for it."

"So was that why he had to stay away from home, because he had to hide after he'd done that shit?"

"Probably."

"Who did he kill?"

George gave her a list. "Plus God knows how many others. I'll know more if Janine catches any gossip at the station once the police access de Luca's file on his laptop. That reminds me, I need to wipe my prints off Lemon's phone and send it to the copshop. It's got a translator app on it so they can decode the information. Fuck's sake, it slipped my mind. I'll do it in a sec."

"I'm thinking of not coming back," she blurted. "Well, I'll have to, to pack my things, hand in my notice, and end the tenancy, but I like it here. I need a fresh start."

"Do you need help with a rent deposit?"

"You've done enough for me already, and you gave me money at Debbie's. Orion's son said we can live with him if we want or rent one of his dad's caravans. But I don't really know him, so maybe I could get a flat."

"Answer me. Do you need a loan? That money I gave you wasn't for a new place."

She sighed. "It would help."

"Then I'll bring it round after your holiday. You have to come back anyway, because Janine's got to be seen as doing her job, dotting the i's and all that shit. She needs to officially tell you Lemon's dead. You know, break the bad news and ask you where you were on the day he died. Easy, because you have an alibi."

"Can she ring me and do it? I'd rather not have coppers at my front door. Actually, I'm surprised my aunt hasn't got in contact about it." She thought of the missed calls that had bleated on her phone throughout the afternoon. "Scrub that, her and Mum have been ringing, but I ignored it."

"Rip the plaster off. Speak to them, get it out of the way now, then enjoy the rest of your holiday. I can give your caravan number to Janine if you like. I don't think they're allowed to give that sort of news over the phone if a copper can do it in person. One of the Southend lot will probably give you a visit."

She pinched the bridge of her nose. "Okay, but let me deal with my mum and Sheila first. Ask Janine to sort it for tomorrow." She gave him her caravan number.

"Fair enough. Now enjoy the rest of your break."

"Um, what will happen about Vanga?"

"If Orion's still the same, he'll have stripped him, burnt his clothes, and washed him in bleach, including inside his mouth, ears, and up his ar—"

"All *right*! I get it."

George smiled. "Later, he'll go out and bury him. Don't even think about it."

"It's hard not to. I never thought I'd kill anyone. It wasn't exactly on my to-do list." Not after what Daksh had done. Not *ever*.

"Oh, come on, you must have entertained suffocating Lemon with a pillow."

She smiled. "Maybe."

George laughed. "Look, I've got to go and sort that bloody phone of his. See you when you get back."

His face disappeared from the screen, and she was left staring at her reflection, surprised she could actually look herself in the eye. She hadn't asked for any of this. Yes, she'd gone running to the twins and set this in motion, but Lemon had been dicing with trouble for a long while, so it seemed, and *he* was responsible for his behaviour, not her.

She opened the caravan door and beckoned for Vernon to come in. Noah sat in his foldaway playpen, waggling a soft rattle then stuffing it in his mouth. Vernon climbed the steps and stared down at him.

"Do you reckon our kids will be as good-looking as him?" he asked.

"Pack it in. I barely know you."

He smiled. "Maybe we should change that."

She smiled back. "Maybe."

Suddenly, she felt revived.

Chapter Twenty-Six

Ruffian stood in the darkness outside Faith Lemon's house and steadied his breathing. Greg had opted to stay at home, saying to be careful, to not get caught—he wasn't in the mood for shenanigans, and Ruffian wasn't in the mood to be told how to suck eggs. Like he'd get caught, Christ…

Faith's area was renowned for the rough element, so it wasn't surprising her son had grown up the way he had, and from what Becky had told them, his mother was a cow of the first order. Still, that rough element, considering George was Ruffian now, might come out of their homes if they spotted him, thinking he was a stranger, and give him some aggro. Not that he was bothered, he could take care of himself, and at a push, he'd tell them The Brothers had sent him, then they'd soon fuck off sharpish. But he didn't need any hassle. He wanted this to be a nice easy job, then he could go home and get some shut-eye. The past few days had knackered him out.

While he waited for his heartbeat to slow so he could concentrate on the work he had to do, he brought to mind the conversation he'd had with Becky at her place when she'd returned from Southend to pack up her belongings, sort out ending her tenancy, and hand in her notice. He'd handed the loan money to her, telling her their terms, but in reality, each time she paid an instalment back, he'd be putting it by for Noah. That little kid had crept into Greg's heart, and George's twin wanted to make sure the boy could go to university if that's what he chose to do. George had agreed, so they'd set up a trust fund.

Ruffian turned and tapped on the front door. Behind the curtains, a light glowed in the downstairs room to his right—Faith likely couldn't sleep, mourning her bastard of a son. The other houses' windows presented as black eyes, shuttered to what was going on outside. Good. Ruffian's earlier musings about the scumbags coming out to speak to him probably wouldn't happen. They were all tucked up in bed, maybe dreaming of where the Sparrow Lot had disappeared to and asking themselves if they could step into their shoes. Earn a bit of dodgy cash selling drugs.

Not fucking likely. We're putting watchmen out on the streets, keeping an eye on things. If anyone puts a foot wrong, they're being hauled in.

With no answer to his knock, Ruffian drummed his gloved fingertips on the window for ages so if Faith was ignoring it, it'd bug her so much she'd *have* to answer. He couldn't blame her for not coming to the door. It was about three a.m., and a woman living alone would be wise not to put herself in danger.

Well, she'd be in danger anyway, because if she didn't fucking hurry up, he'd use his lock pick. Kick the door open if a chain prevented his entry, sod the noise it'd create.

The light in the hallway snapped on, and he smiled. The letterbox flap moved, fingers keeping it propped open.

"Who is it?" a woman asked.

He presumed it was Faith. No reports had come in that she had anyone else in there with her. "I've got a message for you."

"At this time? Post it through the door, then."

"Nah, I've been told to tell you in person." Chuffed at his perfect Scottish accent, Ruffian folded his arms.

"Like I said, who is it?"

"The name's Ruffian."

"What kind of name is *that*?" A pause. "Hold up, are you with the Sparrow Lot?"

"Look, love, just let me in so I can say what I've got to say. I've already done enough overtime as it is. Christ, you're holding me up."

The chain tinkled on the other side—the stupid minger trusted him enough to put herself in the firing line—and the door swung open about five inches, Faith standing in the gap.

He assessed her. White blouse. Beige trousers. Skinny. Dyed black hair. A pinched face. An air about her of not only grief but a hardness he'd seen before. She hadn't led an easy life by the look of her, and he briefly wondered what her story was. Then decided he didn't care *what* she'd been through. Anyone who could be so rude to Becky, so mean, knowing she was desperate for money and help, didn't deserve to have a pretty mug. He hoped her skin scarred so badly it was obvious what had happened to her. He wanted people to know she'd been marked.

"Say whatever it is you came here for, then," she said.

"Och, can't you make me a cuppa while we chat?" He smiled and hoped it swung her into being benevolent, although from what he'd heard, Faith wasn't the kind type. She probably begrudged using one of her teabags on someone other than herself. "Two sugars. Please? It's been a long night."

She studied him. Must have decided he was okay because she stepped back. "I don't want to know if you've come here to tell me stories about my Lemon—the bad kind, I mean."

"I wouldn't do that." Ruffian smiled wider, splitting his thick beard. "You're a heartbroken mother. It'd be cruel if I added to that."

"So you know what he got up to?" She moved farther back as he entered.

"Yeah, but we all make mistakes, don't we." He closed the door. Reached out to take her hand as if he was a good and decent man. Gripped her wrist instead. "Like you."

She frowned, her mind clearly lagging, then she must have realised he'd wheedled his way in under false pretences. "Get out."

"Nah."

He dragged her down the hallway into the kitchen; she fought all the way, scratching at his jacket sleeve and digging her heels in. He flung her towards a table and chairs and chuckled at her crashing into the wall behind them. She raised her fists and turned to face the paintwork.

"I wouldn't bother banging on that if I were you," Ruffian said. "We wouldn't want my bullet to go through it into next door, would we."

She spun round and stared at his raised gun. "What the fuck do you want? Whatever my son did is nothing to do with me."

"So you deny bringing him up to disrespect women?"

"I don't believe he had anything to do with that bunch of perverts. He wouldn't have hurt those poor refugees."

"No, but he was willing to shag them. Women in captivity. What sort of man is that, eh? Not to mention treating Becky like shit."

"Did *she* send you here?"

"I don't take orders, I dish them out. Becky's got fuck all to do with this. Now sit your arse down and listen to me." He tightened his finger on the trigger to shit her up for a laugh.

She rushed forward and took a seat, her hands shaking, her face pale. "L-look, Lemon did some horrible things, so I'm told, but he wouldn't have *meant* it. Whoever killed him must have got the wrong end of the stick. He was a good boy."

"You don't even believe that yourself, so why should I? I can see it in your eyes. You're disappointed in him. Wish he'd turned out differently. But *you* were the one who brought him up. Gave him his values. What did you do, tell him he was the bee's fucking knees? Did you inflate his ego every chance you got?"

"He was all I had. I wanted him to love me, so I did whatever he wanted."

"That's not how parenting works."

"I know that now."

"And going round being horrible to other races isn't how it works either."

"So this *is* about Becky."

"It's about teaching an old bitch that she can't get away with making someone feel like shit. Do you ever stop to think of the damage you're doing? How you make people feel? I've been asking around about you, and the stories weren't great. What was it? How, if you could get away with it, you'd get rid of everyone who wasn't white. You're not a fan of immigrants either, so your little speech back there about the 'poor refugees' is bollocks. You've said they shouldn't have even come here, they don't belong. You're a nasty, sour piece of work, and you're going to learn a lesson on how to keep your spiteful thoughts to yourself."

He took a coil of bungee cord from his pocket and walked behind her. With the safety back on the gun, he popped it in his waistband and looped the cord around her middle, joining the hooks at the back. It reminded him of the ropes when they tied people to the chairs in the warehouse, although she had more freedom of movement. He took another bungee out and secured her wrists, then repeated the action in front on her ankles, waiting for her to kick out or reach forward and snatch at his hair—only it would come off and reveal itself to be a wig. But she sat still, accepting her fate.

"Two blokes have sent me here. You'll be familiar with them, I'm sure. I don't have to say their names—you can work it out. Now, one of them, he has this thing he does, and it shows everyone that he means business, and that the affected person must have done something bad to have him leaving his trademark on them." He stood. "You're going to be one of those people. You'll wear his badge, only he isn't going to be doing the cutting, I am."

That felt weird. Talking as if he were really Ruffian, like he was someone else speaking about George.

He shrugged it off and took the gun from his waistband, pointing it at her. "Why aren't you screaming for help?"

"Because you'll fucking *shoot* me!"

"True." He backed towards the worktop and her magnetic knife stand, all the blades on display. "Which one do you want me to use?"

Her bottom lip wobbled. "What are you talking about?"

"The knives. Which one?"

Her eyelashes fluttered. "Oh God, I know who sent you."

"I bet you do."

"Please, whatever I've done, I'll fix it. Tell them I'll be good. I'll never do anything wrong again."

"I told you what you've done. Do I need to repeat myself?"

"I… Shit. I…"

"You brought up your son to be a wicked bastard. You're a racist. I think that's enough sins, don't you? Or do you want to tell me about some more?"

She shook her head.

"Which. Knife?" he gritted out.

"The… I don't *know*… The shortest one?"

"That won't work. I'll pick." He choose the longest one beside the bread knife—he couldn't be doing with serrated edges, he wanted a clean, fast slice. He slid the gun away. Held the knife up.

Smirked at his ginger reflection. "Now then, try not to make a racket, there's a good girl."

He approached her, and her eyes widened the closer he got. She reared her head back, not that it would do her much good, and he laughed.

"All your chickens are coming home to roost," he said quietly. "They always do, you know. There's no outrunning them. Can you hear them squawking? Flapping their wings?"

She shook her head, staring at him as if he were off his rocker.

She wouldn't be wrong.

"No," she said.

"I can. Loud bastards, so they're angry. They want me to hurt you as much as my friends want me to. Let me give you a bit of advice. The next time you think about spouting nonsense, shut your mouth and think about tonight, whether you want to go through it all over again. I don't mind coming back and slicing through scar tissue, so it's no skin off my nose."

He dragged her chair so the back rested snugly against the wall. Straddled her legs, clamping his to the sides of hers to keep her steady. Positioned the blade on her bottom lip.

"Open wide."

She snorted, and snot landed on the gleaming metal.

"Dirty cow. I *said*, open wide…"

She obeyed—and he knew why. It was pointless not doing as she was told, not when The Brothers had sent someone round to her gaff. She was aware they'd catch up with her again at some point if she drew attention to what he was about to do. Ruffian, pleased that the twins were still feared, smiled.

"I'm not going to lie, this is going to really hurt."

She parted her lips obediently, and he slid the blade farther, stopping just as it bit into the corners of her mouth. Blood welled, and she winced. Whimpered.

"A quick slice, or shall I do it slow?"

She shut her eyes.

"Quick this time," he said, "then if there has to be a repeat performance, I'll take my time. Can say fairer than that, can I."

He pushed the blade to where her gums met at the back, the cheek skin parting, blood running down in sheets to drip onto her white blouse. Somehow, like her son, she managed to keep the noise to a minimum. The apple didn't fall far from the tree, then. Her nostrils flared then stuck flat as she drew air in. A gargle of a whine escaped, and she bunched her eyes tighter.

"Get yourself educated," he said and withdrew the blade. He placed it on the worktop. "Change how you behave, else I'll be back. If my friends hear one whiff that you've told anyone who did this to you, it won't just be a Cheshire smile you end up with. I'll wreck your mush so fucking bad, no one will recognise you. Get yourself to hospital."

He untied her, took the cords with him, and walked out. Paused at the front door. Her sobs filtered through to him, and he examined his feelings. No, not one iota of sympathy. That bitch had it coming to her. Maybe now she'd see the error of her ways. If not, there was always the warehouse.

He strutted outside, whistling, and got in the van, George asking if he could get a shift on because he fancied a Pot Noodle.

Chapter Twenty-Seven

F aith had been trying to come to terms with the loss of her son. And the fact someone had paid her a visit, giving her a Cheshire grin for being racist and bringing Lemon up wrong. It was a George thing to do, everyone knew that, except this bloke had been ginger and Scottish. He'd made her promise to change her ways, to get herself educated, whatever the fuck that meant, and had left her to get herself to the hospital. She was on painkillers, but it still hurt, the skin tight where it was healing. She'd had to lie to the nurse, who'd called the police, and say she'd been attacked down an alley.

Her job…unless a punter liked facial scars, she'd probably lose it.

How had her life turned into…this? A mess. Her, all alone. She'd never imagined she'd be the last one standing. Yet here she was, definitely standing on her doorstep, although she wished she could sit on it. Her legs barely held her up. Her body seemed too heavy, as if grief sat on her shoulders, weighing her down. She leaned on the frame to steady herself, staring down at Noah in his pushchair. The baby slept, oblivious to what his nan was going through, not that she'd ever been a nan to him. She'd spurned the child, hadn't wanted anything to do with him, and she could admit now, that along with him being half black, which hadn't sat well with her *at all*, he reminded her that she was getting older, that all of her dreams might not be within reach anymore.

He'd never remember his father, and even though Faith didn't like to say, maybe that was a good thing. That little boy didn't need a bad influence in his life—Faith had been one to her own child, and the pattern repeating itself didn't bear thinking about. The past didn't need to be churned out again. Lemon had been moulded into who he'd become, she was sure of it. She'd had a big part in it, her mothering ways not the norm; she'd taught him to be selfish and go for what he wanted, fuck everyone else, but someone else had had a hand in his behaviour.

We all make mistakes, but Jesus Christ, I've made some massive ones.

At fifty-two, she was all but on the scrapheap in her opinion, becoming invisible to the crowd. She didn't *want* to be invisible, hence why she opened her mouth and spouted all the crap she did, to be noticed, never forgotten as someone in the midst of menopause and fading from people's best-friend lists. She'd done it to herself, though. In order to survive, to push her past back where it belonged, she'd become someone she'd hate if she met herself on the street.

And she hadn't exactly been kind to Becky, had she?

Faith looked at her. *Pretty girl. Got a lot going for her.*

Becky stood on the path, and she seemed different. *Happy*. At peace. How *could* she be when Lemon had been killed?

Because he was a bastard to her, like Reggie was a bastard to me. When my old man fucked off, wasn't I happy, too?

Or happier. For about a week. She'd felt so free, so giddy with his presence gone, but it hadn't taken long to change. Bitterness had soon made a home inside her, once she knew what it was like to be a single mother. Skint. Always with her hand out until she'd landed the job on another leader's estate, one that paid well, although *she* had to pay as well by selling herself for sex. She never would have thought she'd do that, yet she had, still did.

Maybe that was another reason she'd been nasty to Becky. She saw similarities between them. The single mother. The struggle. Except Faith had resented Becky because she had a good job, a *decent* job, one that no one turned their nose up at.

Faith had lived in dread ever since she'd begun her then-new career. Thinking someone from The Whitehall Estate would come to Cardigan and spot her. Out her. Tell the whole fucking world she was an ageing slag. Who the hell had she thought she was to be so cruel to Becky?

"I'm sorry," she blurted.

Becky's eyes widened. "Didn't think I'd ever hear you say that to me."

"Well, I am. Really sorry. I shouldn't have been so wicked to you."

"No, you shouldn't."

If Faith had the energy, she'd rear back in surprise. It seemed Becky had grown a set—or had found the balls she'd had when she'd first started seeing Lemon.

"I deserved that."

"You did." Becky sighed. "Look, I don't know why I'm bothering, but I'm giving you the courtesy of letting you know that me and Noah are moving away."

Faith nodded. "Someone nipped by this morning to say there was a removal van outside your place."

"Of course they did." Becky rolled her eyes. "All anyone round here knows what to do is gossip."

"Lemon was stupid to insist you both moved into that house. The rent isn't cheap."

"No, which is why it's a puzzle how you could turn me away when I came here begging for help. But it doesn't matter, the twins are dealing with everything for me, so we'll be all right now."

Faith was surprised she didn't have her usual stirring of anger. "It was you?"

Becky frowned. "It was me, what?"

"You told them about me being racist."

Becky shook her head. "Think what you like. I see someone's paid you a visit." She gestured to Faith's face. "You've been racist to others, so it could have been anyone who told them."

"Did you tip the twins off about my Lemon?"

A laugh. "He fucked up all on his own."

Faith studied her for signs of a lie but found nothing to indicate that. Unless Becky had been told to act innocent. The coincidences told a different story. Becky suddenly having enough money to sod off somewhere on holiday. Lemon getting killed. Faith having her face slashed. The Brothers didn't usually deposit dead bodies, though, they got rid of them, so perhaps they hadn't had anything to do with Lemon's death. Maybe Becky hadn't done anything but borrow a few quid off them.

Lemon in mind, Faith said, "Silly boy."

"Arsehole, more like. Anyway, I'll send you pictures of Noah as he's growing up, maybe nip round here when I'm back in London seeing my mum and dad."

Faith jolted. "You're moving out of *London*?"

"Yes. New start, away from what I've discovered can be a cesspit of hatred. I assume you *want* pictures of Noah? I mean, you've told me enough times you don't think he's Lemon's. There's always a DNA test if you want to go down that road."

"Pictures would be lovely." Faith forced herself to show she was grateful by saying, "Thank you." But it stung. To grovel to a black woman.

Stop it. Stop thinking like that.

Her face itched, as if to remind her of what would happen if she didn't get her thoughts in check.

Becky stared up the street at a lamppost on the corner. She seemed miles away, as if remembering something. She shook her head. "Well, we're off. Not sure when we'll next be back, but I'll text you and check if you want me to pop round. I won't just turn up."

"Where are you going?"

"I'd rather not say."

Becky walked off, pushing a piece of Lemon away, the little baby Faith had promised herself she'd love now her son was gone, but how could she show that if Becky was taking him to God knew where?

As usual, life had handed Faith lemons, and she laughed wryly at the irony. First Reggie had been given to her, then her son, then Noah. All now snatched away.

Maybe I ought to get my head out of my arse and make some lemonade.

She shut the door. Her phone rang on the side in the kitchen, and she rushed to answer it, momentarily thinking it would be Lemon, then she remembered he was gone. A wave of grief swept over her, and she reached for the mobile, all emotions to do with mourning flashing away to be replaced with anxiety. Her son's death had erased some of her previous life, the dread she'd been feeling just before he'd passed away. How she'd worried she'd get in the shit and muck up what that man wanted her to do. Did she have to do it now?

Yes, she did. She couldn't have the neighbours looking down their noses at her—the man had threatened to tell everyone what she did for a living if she didn't obey him, plus she needed the money so she could move away herself. Real life had slammed right back, and she had to deal with yet another shitstorm.

She read the message.

IT'S A GO. GET YOUR ARSE TO WORK AND DO WHAT I TOLD YOU. IF YOU DON'T…WELL, YOU KNOW HOW MUCH I LIKE STRANGLING PEOPLE, DON'T YOU…

She felt sick.

Fuck.

To be continued in *Rebirth*,
The Cardigan Estate 22

Printed in Great Britain
by Amazon

27725845R00219